What Dreams May Fall

a novel by Alana Terry

"When you walk through the fire, you will not be burned; the flames will not set you ablaze."

Isaiah 43:2

Note: The views of the characters in this novel do not necessarily reflect the views of the author, nor is their behavior necessarily condoned.

The characters in this book are fictional. Any resemblance to real persons is coincidental. No part of this book may be reproduced in any form (electronic, audio, print, film, etc.) without the author's written consent.

What Dreams May Fall

Copyright © 2018 Alana Terry

March, 2018

Cover design by Cover Mint Designs.

Scriptures quoted from THE HOLY BIBLE, NEW INTERNATIONAL VERSION®, NIV® Copyright © 1973, 1978, 1984, 2011 by Biblica, Inc.® Used by permission. All rights reserved worldwide.

www.alanaterry.com

CHAPTER 1

The leaves rustled in the trees, a sure sign of autumn.

Ruby stood up from the table and stretched. Time to get back to work. She smiled at her employer. "Thanks for the cinnamon rolls."

"Well now." Connie bustled to the table to clear Ruby's dishes. "If Grandma Lucy's still asleep and doesn't need anything, you're welcome to sit a spell longer and keep me company. My back's about wore out, milking all those goats today. Care for a game of cards?"

Ruby smiled. She had never worked for a kinder woman. God must have heard her when she asked him for a better job than her position as a floor nurse at County Hospital.

It was the first real answer to prayer she'd experienced in the few months she'd been a Christian. She got up from the table after promising a round of rummy later. Connie's son had recently moved to Costa Rica to become a full-time missionary, and she knew Connie was starved for company.

Ruby was hired to take care of Connie's aunt, but when Grandma Lucy was having a good day, Ruby spent more time keeping Connie company in the kitchen than she did using her nursing degree. She loved her new job. Grandma Lucy had been the one to lead Ruby to Christ when Ruby was stitching up her forehead at County Hospital last summer. It was hard to imagine how different her life would be if Grandma Lucy hadn't fallen that night. So many things had improved on the one hand.

On the other …

Ruby's cell phone chimed to sound off an incoming text.

Free tonight? Movies in Wenatchee. I'll pick you up at five. Girls' night only.

Ruby stared at the message from her best friend. She and Jessi had known each other since kindergarten, walked with each other through every major life event, including Ruby's graduation from nursing school and her mother's battle with cancer. Even though Jessi was as staunch an atheist as Ruby had been just a few months ago, she never made Ruby feel bad for converting.

Never turned her back on her.

If only the same could be said about others …

Ruby shook her head. She didn't need to wallow in self-pity. She shot a quick text back to Jessi.

We'll see. Might have to stay late to help with dinner.

There was no way to guess if Grandma Lucy would wake up from her afternoon nap with enough energy to preach at Ruby for three hours straight, mixing heavy doses of prayer into her sermons, or if she'd be so out of it she'd start asking for her dead ex-husband.

It was painful for Ruby to see her in that condition. The night they met, Grandma Lucy had appeared so strong. So powerful. That's what had drawn Ruby toward her in the first place. While getting her forehead stitched up, Grandma Lucy spoke as if she'd known about all of Ruby's secret longings, the late nights she spent wondering if there was any higher purpose in a universe that appeared so chaotic.

Ruby still couldn't explain how the transformation had happened so quickly. So thoroughly. Grandma Lucy said that was just how the Holy Spirit worked, but what Grandma Lucy didn't understand was how Ruby had been antagonistic to any idea of religion for so many years. Even her best friend Jessi, who once jokingly purchased an ordination certificate from an online atheist "church," would have been more likely to turn to Christianity than Ruby.

What had this old woman done to her?

And if Ruby had the opportunity to do it all over again,

knowing what she would lose, realizing what she would have to give up if she gave her life to Christ, would she make the same decision twice?

CHAPTER 2

"Time to wake up." Ruby touched Grandma Lucy's shoulder. The old woman looked so tiny when she slept, like a white-haired toddler taking her afternoon nap.

"Grandma Lucy?" she repeated.

"What time is it?" she mumbled.

Ruby held her breath. The next ten seconds would be the decisive ones, the time it took for Ruby to find out if Grandma Lucy would be herself and quote Bible verses all evening from her prayer chair or if she'd spend the night confused and weak, unable to remember her niece who'd lived with her for so many years, asking about relatives who'd been dead and gone for decades.

Before he ran off to become a missionary, Connie's son took Grandma Lucy to some place in Seattle, a memory clinic specializing in dementia, but at the time of her appointment Grandma Lucy had been completely lucid. She claimed divine healing. The day Ruby started working at Safe Anchorage Farm just a few months later, Grandma

Lucy didn't even remember the night she got her stitches.

Grandma Lucy sat up in bed with a groan. "Why's my back hurt?"

"You've probably been lying down too long without rolling over. You want to get in your wheelchair?"

She shook her head. "No, take me to my prayer chair. I've got some things to talk to God about."

Even when Grandma Lucy forgot her own children, she knew that her life's greatest work was to rock away in that sitting room, praying for loved ones whose names she couldn't even recall.

"We'll go to your prayer room soon," Ruby told her. "But first, let's go use the bathroom, and then Connie made you a little snack to have with your medicine."

Oops. She shouldn't have said that.

Grandma Lucy shook her thinning head of white hair. "No medicine. I feel fine."

Ruby had learned not to argue. "All right. Well, how about a cinnamon roll?"

Grandma Lucy's face lit up like a preschooler's on Christmas morning. "Now you're talking." She rubbed her hands together. "I love cinnamon rolls. Did Mom make them?"

Ruby was busy putting the brakes on Grandma Lucy's

wheelchair and didn't answer.

"They smell delicious." Grandma Lucy inhaled deeply, even though Connie had been working at the Safe Anchorage gift shop and hadn't cooked a thing since yesterday, when she'd spent the entire morning cooking to prepare for Grandma Lucy's upcoming birthday party. "There's nothing like fresh bread rolls straight from the oven. You smell that yeast?"

Ruby nodded and wheeled the chair up to the bedside. "It will be delicious, I'm sure."

Grandma Lucy cocked her head, and Ruby guessed what she was going to ask even before she said the words. "Is that you, Nora?"

She didn't have the heart to remind Grandma Lucy her daughter Nora had been killed by a drunk driver decades earlier. "No, I'm Ruby. I'm the nurse you led to Jesus at County Hospital."

"Really?" Grandma Lucy looked pensive. "So we've known each other a while?"

"Just a few months. I started coming over for tea and prayer, remember? You'd sit in your rocking chair and teach me about Jesus."

Grandma Lucy nodded. "Did you know that when a sinner repents, even the angels in heaven rejoice?"

"You're the one who taught me that. Come on. Let's get you out of bed."

Grandma Lucy was lighter than the bulky wheelchair. She didn't need it always, but with her memory acting up, Ruby didn't want her trying the walker. Not today.

"Thank you." Grandma Lucy's voice was soft when she patted Ruby's hand. "Aren't you a sweet thing to help out an old woman like this. What's your name?"

"I'm Ruby." It was a good thing Ruby had babysat and nannied her way through nursing school. All that work with children had given her a heavy dose of patience.

Grandma Lucy continued to pat Ruby's hand. "And are you a born-again believer, Ruby? Do you know the Lord Jesus as your personal Savior?"

"I do. You're the one who taught me." *Remember?* she was about to say but stayed quiet and wheeled the chair toward the door.

"Where did you say we're going?" Grandma Lucy asked.

"Into the kitchen to get a snack."

Grandma Lucy inhaled loudly. "Well, it smells delicious. Did Mom make bread rolls?"

CHAPTER 3

"I'm telling you, girl," Jessi exclaimed as she sped with Ruby toward Wenatchee, "we totally need to get you out more. This is the first time you've left that farm in what, like a month?"

Ruby rubbed her throbbing temples.

"Headache again?"

Ruby shrugged, downplaying her discomfort. "Just a little one. It's not too bad."

"How many headaches did you get when you were still working at County?"

Ruby didn't answer.

"So I heard from Mace yesterday." Jessi glanced at Ruby out of the corner of her eye. Ruby wished she'd keep her focus on the road.

Jessi drummed a little beat on her steering wheel. "Sounds like he's got a pretty light semester, which is perfect for him. I honestly have no idea how he's made it this far already."

Some people might not find it all that much of an accomplishment to be a sixth-year senior who hadn't flunked out of college yet, but Jessi's brother Mace was a special case.

Ruby didn't reply.

Jessi glanced over at her. "What's wrong? You're like a fish out of water after it's done flopping."

Ruby tried to straighten down her windblown hair. It could be the middle of winter, and Jessi would still be driving with the windows down. "I'm just tired."

"That old quack have another one of her bad days?"

Ruby tensed. *I will not get into another fight with Jessi,* she repeated to herself like a prayer.

Jessi shrugged. "Well, I swear I'd trade you jobs any day of the week. Tell you what, those little brats at the daycare are always screaming so loud that I come home with a migraine every night."

Ruby knew for a fact her best friend had never suffered a migraine in her entire life but didn't want to argue.

We will not get into another fight.

Jessi groaned dramatically. "And then there's all the older kids coming in the afternoons now, bringing home all their back-to-school germs and everything else. I swear I've caught five different colds in the past week."

Ruby didn't point out the medical implausibility of her statement. *We will not get into another fight.*

"Anyway, Mace seems to be settling in well. I swear, it's not fair that he got all the brains in the family but he's wasting it all just to party hard in Spokane. I'm twice the worker he is, and what have I got to show for it? A stupid associate's degree that means squat and a job at a snot factory." She swatted Ruby's leg playfully. "Come on. I'm talking to you. What are you thinking about?"

"Just Grandma Lucy."

Jessi snorted. "That old bat? Seriously, you know I'm only saying this because you're my absolute best friend in the entire world and we've gone through literally everything together, but this woman has kind of got you bewitched. Know what I mean?"

We will not get into another fight, Ruby repeated to herself while Jessi continued talking over the roar of the wind outside.

"Seriously. Like one minute you're just your normal, average self. And by average I don't mean average like that. I'm just saying you're who you've always been, then you come home from one little night shift at County and tell me you're giving this whole Jesus thing a try, and you know me. I was like, *hey that's awesome, whatever tickles your goat,* know what I mean? But then next thing I know, you're going over to her house to spend time talking about who knows what, then you're breaking up with my brother …"

"Mace didn't have anything to do with this," Ruby snapped, forgetting her well-rehearsed mantra.

Thankfully, Jessi was too absorbed in her own soliloquy to argue. "I mean, hooray Jesus and all, I hear he's got some really awesome things to teach us about loving each other and stuff, and wasn't Gandhi sort of like a Christian? Like not a *Christian* Christian because I think he was a Hindu, or maybe it was Buddhist, I don't know. But I mean, I think he read a lot of Jesus' teachings and stuff, so hey, if it's good for Gandhi, it's gotta be good for all of us, right? But you're kind of carrying it a little far, don't you think?"

"I don't know," Ruby mumbled. Why did she have to live in a small town like Orchard Grove, where if you wanted to get any real entertainment you had to drive at least an hour and a half to arrive anywhere?

Jessi took in a deep breath before jumping into the next round of her monologue. "I mean, you remember when I got all into those billionaire romance novels, and you finally told me I was wasting my brain cells? And I listened to you, right? Or that summer I thought it'd be cool to start smoking but you talked me out of it before I got too addicted? That's what friends do for each other, right? You think it was fun listening to you tell me how degrading those novels are about women getting beat up and slapped around? But you stood your ground, and I eventually came to realize you were right. Out go my trashy romances, or at least most of them. Next you tell me you'll never let me ride in your car if I smell like smoke. Out go the cigarettes before I ruin my lungs and die of cancer. Because that's what friends do." She enunciated each word with even more melodrama than normal.

"So think of this as your own personal intervention." While her best friend railed on, Ruby just wished she could tune out her words. Jessi didn't know what that first conversation with Grandma Lucy did to her, how much hope it poured into her soul. Jessi didn't know about how much Ruby had been struggling until that night at County. She didn't know how far Ruby had slipped into despondency and despair, how lonely she felt even when she was surrounded by friends.

Grandma Lucy had changed everything.

No, Jesus had changed everything.

Why couldn't Jessi be happy for her and leave it at that?

"I'm not telling you to stop believing. I'm just like the Journey song. It's not my place to decide what you're supposed to think about God or religion or anything like that.

That's totally against everything I stand for. And hey, if this whole church-girl act is working out for you, all the more power to you. But isn't it the Bible that says *everything in moderation*? No wait, maybe that was Gandhi. Or Martin Luther King. I forget now, but that's beside the point, although now that I think about it, wasn't King a Christian too? So I mean, yeah, let's be all for team Jesus if that's what's working for you now. But I've always said religion's like underwear. Some people like boy boxers, and some go for the bikini briefs. If you're going on a hot date you might choose something with a lot of lace, and then there are people who go totally commando, and that's perfectly fine too as long as you don't go announcing what you're wearing to the world, right? Like those desperate girls who wear a thong with their hip huggers. Get what I'm saying?"

"Not really," Ruby mumbled.

"I'm just saying that some things like your underwear and your religion are between you and the washing machine and not too many other folks. Unless of course we're talking about that hot date. Which brings me to my last point."

Ruby rubbed her throbbing temples. *Not Mace. Please don't bring up Mace.*

"You and my brother. You two have been destined for each other since the day we all met. You know that, right?"

Ruby should have known Jessi wouldn't shy away from bringing him into this very one-sided conversation.

"And we promised each other when the two of you started dating — again — that no matter what happened with you and Mace, it wouldn't get in the way of our friendship, the whole *sisters before misters* thing and all that. I hate to put it this way, but you kind of sort of broke his heart. And you know me. I'm not one to be melodramatic or anything, but he was pretty devastated by it all."

Ruby shook her head. Whatever Jessi thought it was that had split her and Mace up, she was wrong.

Dead wrong.

She grabbed Jessi's cell phone and plugged it into the car speakers. "I'm really tired. Mind if we just listen to some music for a while?"

"Be my guest." Jessi shrugged, and Ruby turned on their favorite 80s rock playlist.

Two minutes later, Jessi was shouting *Don't Stop Believing* at the top of her not-quite-so-musical lungs, and Ruby was leaning back in her seat, praying her headache would go away, wondering if she'd made a mistake to hang out with Jessi tonight in the first place.

CHAPTER 4

Ruby woke up the next morning, her headache just as fierce as before. When Connie asked her to quit her job at County to take care of Grandma Lucy, it took time to warm up to the idea. Ruby had never done in-home nursing before, and she wasn't sure how much she loved the idea of living where she worked. There were financial considerations too. Connie agreed to pay her out of pocket for the first two months while they waited for all the insurance paperwork to get filed, but if the state came back and decided Grandma Lucy wasn't sick enough to require round-the-clock care, Connie couldn't afford to pay her indefinitely. If Ruby had been searching for financial security, she would have never left County.

On the other hand, she had grown to love Grandma Lucy, the eccentric old woman who had led her to Christ. On her good days, Ruby was basically paid to sit and learn more about Jesus, and when Grandma Lucy wasn't as lucid, Ruby was happy to repay the favor by watching over her.

She'd had a hard time making up her mind back then, but once she and Mace broke up, there wasn't much choice unless she wanted to bunk up with Jessi. Close as the two girls were and had always been, they'd tried the roommate thing their first semester of college and vowed to never put their friendship through such a strain again.

Fortunately, after moving into the small attic room at Safe Anchorage's bright red farmhouse, she realized how much she appreciated the convenience of getting out of bed and being ready for work by the time she made her way downstairs.

Of course, living with her employer also made it more difficult to separate work from pleasure, which is why she appreciated her nights out with Jessi. Until Jessi spent the entire ride both to and from Wenatchee lecturing her about her new faith in Jesus.

Oh, well. At least they were still talking. Ruby had been afraid when she and Mace broke up that she might lose Jessi too. She was thankful that her fears were unfounded, but she still longed for simpler times when it was her and Mace and Jessi all together, staying up until two or three in the morning drinking coffee and playing stupid board games or driving around Orchard Grove like they were high schoolers again, looking for parties to crash.

On her way to the bathroom, Ruby stopped at the sound of a familiar voice coming from the greenhouse attachment that had long ago been converted into Grandma Lucy's personal prayer room. Ruby lost count of how many nights Grandma Lucy had tried to make it to her prayer room, risking broken bones and fractured hips just to sit in her rocking chair. Sometimes Ruby wondered why Connie didn't let her just sleep there. Wouldn't it make things that much easier?

The lights were on, so Ruby poked her head inside. Grandma Lucy was rocking so hard it was a miracle momentum didn't throw her out of the chair. She was covered with her favorite prayer quilt, her hands raised toward heaven.

"Lord, you are the God of the ages, the Lord of hosts, the King of the universe. There isn't a single sparrow that falls to the ground apart from your will, not a single word on our tongues that you do not know. You have searched me and you know me. You know when I sit and when I rise. You raise me up to soar with eagle's wings so that my youth is renewed like the dew of heaven. You feed me your holy manna, you fill me with your sacred Word, you anoint me with your Holy Spirit.

"My mind is yours, gracious Father, and even though the

devil wants to keep me in confusion, you are a God of order and discipline. I declare that I am not a slave again to fear, but you have given me a sound mind so that I may know and testify to what you have done. Even the darkness will not be dark to me. The night will shine like the day, for dark is light to you, and I am convinced that no weapon forged against me will prevail." She balled her hand into a fist.

"You hear that, old devil you? This old mind of mine belongs to the Lord, and you can't take away my clarity. Not today. For greater is he who is in me than he who is in the world, and even the demons shudder at the powerful and holy name of Jesus Christ, the Lamb of God, who takes away the sins of the world. And did you sleep well last night? You're certainly up early, aren't you?"

It took Ruby far longer than it should have to realize Grandma Lucy was staring straight at her.

She stepped into the room. "Hi, Grandma Lucy. Are you having a good morning today?"

She chuckled. "Any morning spent in prayer is a good morning."

Ruby glanced at the clock. "How long have you been here?"

"Not long. Just a few hours, I'd guess. I'd normally go out to the goats. That's where I used to pray at night so I wouldn't bother anyone else, but you know, Connie's put that contraption on the doorknob, and I can't for the life of me figure out how it works. I know four foreign languages, but I can't figure out a simple baby lock." She laughed softly. "Guess Connie wants to keep me from freezing my tail off outside, is that it?"

"We just don't want to see you get hurt."

Grandma Lucy's eyes twinkled. "Well, that's sweet of you, I'm sure, but what would have happened if I hadn't taken that fall and needed stitches in my forehead? What then? You wouldn't have sewn me up so good, I would have never had the chance to share such joyous news as the gospel with you, and you'd probably still be working at that hospital, doing your night shifts, going home to that atheist boyfriend you were with …"

"Are you hungry?" Ruby interrupted. "I think Connie's making some cinnamon rolls."

"I know. I've been smelling them rise for the past hour or two. Makes my mouth water so much I'm just about to die of thirst."

"Well, let me get your wheelchair, and then we'll find you a glass of something to drink."

Grandma Lucy shook her head. "Nope. I won't be needing that chair today. Not after God's touched my body and made me strong."

Ruby took a step forward. "Your walker then. You stay there, and I'll go get it."

Grandma Lucy scowled. "Now, what have we been talking about when we pray together each afternoon? If the Son has set you free, he'll make you free indeed, right? So what kind of witness would I be to you if I allowed you to get me some contraption to help me walk even after Jesus Christ himself has ministered to my spirit and made me strong?"

"I know you're strong. I just think you should get your …" Ruby jumped forward as Grandma Lucy stood up, holding onto the unsteady arm of her rocker for support. Her knee buckled, and Ruby reached her hand out to guide her gently back into the chair, bracing her foot against it to keep it from sliding.

Grandma Lucy looked up sheepishly. "Did I ever tell you the verse that says pride cometh before the fall?"

Ruby tried to offer a comforting smile, and Grandma Lucy whispered in a voice half her usual volume, "Maybe that wheelchair isn't a bad idea after all."

CHAPTER 5

"Grandma Lucy, do you want another cinnamon roll?" Connie asked. "I made plenty to get ready for your birthday party."

It had taken Ruby a few weeks living here to realize that Connie had and always would preside over mealtimes. Ruby's only job was to eat as much of Connie's homemade cooking as possible and help Grandma Lucy cut her food if necessary.

"Got the morning news?" Connie's husband asked, handing her yesterday's paper with one hand and reaching out for the new one with his other. Ruby had been living here for months and couldn't remember a single time Connie's husband had spoken directly to her.

"It's going to be a special day." Connie was still standing, which wasn't in the least unusual. By Ruby's best approximation, Connie sat down during a meal once or twice a week and never for more than two or three minutes.

"More coffee?" she asked her husband, already standing

over him with the pot in hand.

He grunted and held up his mug.

"So," Connie continued with her announcement, "I'll be at the gift shop this morning working on some plans for Grandma Lucy's birthday party, then after lunch we're having that nice young man from Seattle come by. Remember him, Grandma Lucy? He called a few days ago and said the two of you had a good talk about the Lord."

"Of course. You're talking about Elliot, the cancer doctor, right?"

Connie smiled proudly. "You remembered. That's good."

"He'd be a hard one to forget. That young man is hurting. I've been praying for him every day since we met in Seattle. It was when I went in for those silly memory tests, and Elliot was there in the cafeteria, and I just knew God was telling me to go over there and talk to him." She shook her head. "Such a hard, sad life."

Ruby wasn't sure she'd ever get used to these strange, random visitors who stopped by Safe Anchorage, people who had run into Grandma Lucy weeks or months or sometimes even years ago to tell her how she'd led them to Christ or how God had answered some special prayer she'd prayed for them. For a retired missionary, she was certainly still letting God use her to lead people to salvation. Last year, Grandma Lucy had fallen so ill the doctors thought she was going to die in the hospital, so she recorded a video urging every last one of her friends and family members who weren't yet saved to accept Jesus into their hearts. Connie had shown it to Ruby one night. The message gave her chills.

"I'm just so thankful you're having a good day," Connie said, pouring more tea into Grandma Lucy's cup.

Grandma Lucy smiled. "It's always a good day when the Lord's in control."

Ruby didn't say anything. Did Grandma Lucy recall that yesterday she'd forgotten Ruby's name? That she thought her mom was still alive baking bread rolls in Connie's kitchen?

Nobody around the table seemed to have the heart to tell her.

Connie wiped her hands on the sides of her checkered apron and gave a big smile. "Well now, who's hungry for more rolls?"

CHAPTER 6

Elliot Jameson couldn't remember the last time he was this nervous. *It's just a simple, informal visit,* he told himself as he made his way down the winding dirt road.

He hoped his GPS wasn't steering him wrong. He'd had no idea Orchard Grove was this small a town until he got here.

Nearly four months had passed since he first met that fiery old woman with her white hair. He had been finishing up an eighteen-hour shift. All he'd wanted was a quick fruit salad then a few hours' sleep before he came back to start it all over again.

It was the life of a resident. The life he'd chosen.

If it hadn't been for that bold little lady making her way to his table, he'd be home now. Enjoying his day off. Sleeping in past five in the morning. Catching up on his reading. Restocking the veggie compartment of his fridge. Maybe taking a walk in the fresh autumn air.

Not driving out to the tiniest little town on the

Washington state map, subjecting his newly leased Tesla to this bumpy dirt road, all to sit in some old woman's dining room to ask her about one of his oncology patients. Charis was still a young mother. She'd gone through the treatments, subjected her body to multiple rounds of chemo and radiation, and in the end all she ended up with was a bald head and a tumor twice the size it had been when she was diagnosed four months earlier.

Aggressive. That's what the cancer was. Like that one foster dad who'd whipped Elliot with his belt because he assumed his asthma and thick-rimmed glasses meant he was gay. Elliot hadn't fully understood what the word meant until the man tried to beat it out of him. The next day at school it was a label that stuck until he changed districts.

Kids were cruel. That's why Elliot could have never gone into teaching like his fiancée Amy. She was a kindergarten teacher, loved by all her kids. He'd been thinking about her far more than usual today. Maybe it was the long drive. When was the last time he'd been alone for hours with just his thoughts?

All to see some crazy old woman and ask her how it was that her prayer had healed his most hopeless patient.

How it was that a tumor so large could just disappear.

It might make more sense if Grandma Lucy had gone

into the room and prayed for Charis while she was awake and lucid. If Charis knew that she'd been prayed for, maybe there could be some sort of placebo effect that could explain the impossible. Elliot had spent the past several weeks perusing the medical journals for every study he could find on prayer and healing. Some of the first reports showed direct connections, but most of these early tests had been called into question. And what about that one study where the group who got prayed over actually experienced a longer recovery time than the control?

It was fringe science at best. Yet Charis's charts and x-rays and scans were right there for anyone to see. He and the oncology team had puzzled over them in the conference room more than once. If Elliot hadn't run the tests himself, he might have thought they scanned the wrong patient, but this wasn't a case of simple human error.

So what was it?

He passed a sign for Safe Anchorage Farms. At least he was on the right road. He'd need to find a car wash on the way out of this little town. His Tesla had never taken such a beating. He kept his windows rolled up. Usually, his asthma was completely under control. He only used his inhaler every few months and had gone years since his last real attack, but he didn't need all that dust blowing up and getting into his lungs.

Smelly Elly scratched his belly, couldn't breathe so down he fell-y.

Why in the world would he be thinking about childhood taunts from twenty years ago? And what kind of kid was stupid enough, mean enough, to make fun of someone for having asthma?

That's what he loved about Amy. She made sure that no child in her class felt bullied or belittled — by kids or adults. She was this tiny, five-foot-two bundle of love and gentleness, but she'd go head-to-head with the most belligerent of parents and never think about backing down.

He missed her so much.

You'd laugh if you saw me now, he thought. Ironically, Amy had always been the more spiritual one, the one who pushed him to go to church even when he was exhausted from his studies. She was the one who called him up to pray with him before every single major test he took in med school.

She died two weeks before he took his last final, and he was terrified that he wouldn't be able to pass.

You left me far too soon.

He sighed. It had been her idea to wait until after he graduated to get married. She was convinced that he was going to become this world-renowned doctor, single-handedly saving the lives of millions, and she didn't want to distract him from that goal. He would have been happy marrying her the first summer they met. She had laughed and insisted there was no reason to rush. They had all the time in the world.

It wasn't fair.

He hadn't told Grandma Lucy any of this when they talked in the hospital cafeteria so many months ago, but even then, she'd acted like she'd known. Elliot was far too busy to have any sort of social media presence. The woman couldn't even remember his name from the start of their ten-minute conversation to the end, and yet her words made him almost certain she knew about Amy.

But how?

He slammed on his brakes when some kind of animal bounded across the road. Was that a goat?

He rolled down a long driveway, never topping five miles an hour. His leased car was a lavish expenditure, ridiculously above his salary as a resident, but he lived simply enough in other areas of his life to make up for it. If he had known how rural this country drive would be, he would have rethought his plans. But at least he was here.

He parked the car and glanced around. On the right was

a building labeled Safe Anchorage Gift Shop. On the left was a two-story farmhouse, fire-engine red. A plump, smiling woman bustled out of the house as he stepped out of his Tesla.

"You must be Dr. Jameson. Grandma Lucy will be so tickled you came all the way out from Seattle to visit."

"Call me Elliot." He studied the area. This was exactly the type of home he dreamed of growing up in when he was new enough to the foster system that he still hoped to find a permanent home.

The woman threw her arms around him. She smelled like hay and cinnamon. "Come in. Grandma Lucy's having a good day, thank the Lord. I think it's going to be a wonderful visit."

Elliot wasn't sure what she meant by *a good day*, yet another reminder that he was here to see a complete stranger. He was probably making a terrible fool out of himself, but he'd driven so far and was already here.

The woman in the apron beckoned him into the farmhouse.

He had no idea what he was getting himself into, but since there was nothing worse than uncertainty, he stepped forward and followed her in.

CHAPTER 7

Ruby was in the bedroom with Grandma Lucy when Connie bustled in from outside.

"Welcome to Safe Anchorage Farms, where you come in as a friend and walk out as family."

Connie's spiel to visitors always bugged Ruby. It sounded like she was trying to initiate them into some sort of cult.

"Is that Brad out there?" Grandma Lucy asked. She had spilled some tea down her blouse at lunch, and Ruby was helping her change.

"I think it's the doctor you met in Seattle," Ruby answered. "Brad's in Costa Rica, remember?" She'd met Connie's son briefly the night he brought Grandma Lucy into the hospital to get those stitches, but he'd been out of the country by the time Ruby started working at Safe Anchorage.

Grandma Lucy shook her head. "I told Brad I don't need to see any more doctors. God's healed me, and if the Son sets you free, you are free indeed."

"I know." Ruby buttoned up the collar of Grandma Lucy's clean blouse. "He's not here to check you out. You're not his patient. This is just a visit. He wants to talk to you."

Ruby hoped Grandma Lucy wouldn't become forgetful again, not after starting the day off so strong.

She smiled. "That's right. The young man who takes care of cancer patients. The one I went to talk to in the cafeteria because God told me how sad he was."

Ruby nodded. "You remember."

"Of course I do. I've been praying for that young man every single day since we met, praying for him and a patient he was particularly concerned about. Now he's here, you say?"

"Yeah. Connie just let him in."

"Connie?" Grandma Lucy looked surprised.

Ruby hoped the dementia wasn't making its way back. Not right now. The last thing she wanted was for Grandma Lucy to start asking after her mother or her dead ex.

"Yeah. Connie. Your niece."

Grandma Lucy chuckled. "I know who she is. But she said she'd be working at the gift shop today. Right there at the breakfast table. I heard her, sure as Mary heard the angel Gabriel."

"Oh, yeah. Well, either way, he's here. Are you ready to go meet your company?"

Grandma Lucy furrowed her brow. "I most certainly am not."

Ruby was about to ask why. Was Grandma Lucy embarrassed to use her walker? Had she stopped feeling well all of a sudden? Before she could figure out what was wrong, Grandma Lucy interrupted her thoughts with a prayer.

"Father God, this is a young man who is broken and hurting. This is a young man desperately yearning for your loving touch. You see what he needs. You understand the sorrows he carries. You long to lift his burdens, Lord. Use my words to bring healing, comfort, and peace today. Amen."

Ruby wondered if she would ever get used to those spontaneous prayers. Could Grandma Lucy at least give some sort of a warning?

Grandma Lucy straightened herself up to her full four feet eleven inches and gave a regal tilt of her head. "I'm ready," she said and waited for Ruby to open the bedroom door.

CHAPTER 8

"You'll have to excuse Grandma Lucy," Connie said. "She'll be here in just a minute, I'm sure."

Elliot had never seen someone bustle around so busily. He was almost dizzy just watching her. After seating him at the dining room table Connie brought over a plate of cinnamon rolls, a jug of lemonade, a tray of fruit, and a bowl of homemade yogurt. "This is straight from our goats. Nothing better for your gut than fresh goat yogurt."

Elliot took a bite. "That's good."

"You think so? Now, some people say it's too bitter because I don't do anything other than add a little bit of honey."

"It's great. I like it like that." Elliot wondered if Safe Anchorage was strictly local or if they'd consider supplying the health food store where he shopped in Seattle.

Connie stared down the hall with her hand on her hip and a frown on her face. "Maybe I should see what's going on with Grandma Lucy. I hope she's not giving Ruby any trouble back there."

"Who's Ruby?" It was a name he hadn't heard in years.

"Oh, didn't I tell you about her yet? In fact, I'm sure I did. On the telephone, that's right. Ruby's the nurse who got saved stitching up Grandma Lucy's head when she fell last summer."

Elliot stared at the tree outside the kitchen window. "Ruby's the nurse?" He remembered the story about how Grandma Lucy found her live-in help, but he was certain he would have remembered if anyone had mentioned the name Ruby.

And she was a nurse.

"Are you all right, hon? You look hot. Should I prop open a window? Would that make you more comfortable?"

Elliot didn't answer. His focus was fixed on the young woman walking down the hall toward him. He jumped out of his chair, grateful he didn't topple it over.

"Ruby?"

She stared. It was as if time paused, and he could read each changing reaction that mirrored his own.

The surprise.

Then disbelief.

Followed by a painful, searing embarrassment.

CHAPTER 9

Ruby had to stop acting like a fool. She was a professional. An adult. Connie was paying her a decent wage to live here and take care of Grandma Lucy, not to run away when things got uncomfortable.

She replayed everything she'd heard Grandma Lucy and Connie say about her visitor. *Oncology doctor. Resident. Young man from Seattle.*

She was blind not to have suspected. If she'd known, she would have taken the day off. But it was too late now.

She squared her shoulders and forced herself to stare straight into his eyes. "Hello, Dr. Jameson. Nice to see you again."

"You can call me Elliot."

Connie clasped her hands in front of her. "So you know each other?" Her face was so bright it could have rivaled last night's harvest moon. "That's wonderful. Isn't this a small world? Don't you just love when God brings people together when they least expect it?"

Ruby didn't answer. She would make sure Grandma Lucy was comfortable, then she'd find something to keep herself busy as far from here as possible.

She pulled out a chair and helped Grandma Lucy into her seat, fully aware that Elliot was staring at her, trying to get her attention as if he might deliver some sort of telepathic message.

Whatever it was, she didn't want to hear it.

She cleared her throat and spoke more loudly than normal. "Do you need anything else, Grandma Lucy, or are you all set?"

Grandma Lucy held her hand. "I'm fine. Bless you for all the kindness you show me, and bless you for the ministry God's granted you to use your gifts of compassion and service to watch over an old soul like mine."

Sweet and flowery and well-intentioned as her words might be, Ruby was ready for Grandma Lucy to cut the niceties short. After all, Ruby was only going to her room. Not nearly far enough, but it was the best she could do.

She gave a curt nod, checked to make sure her cell was in her pocket, and excused herself, taking the stairs up to her attic room two at a time.

CHAPTER 10

Why had he come here? This whole trip had been a mistake. Elliot saw that clearly now.

Connie finished serving up their plates and then wiped her hands on her apron. "Well, I'm going to go check on things over at the gift shop, and I'll leave you two together to talk. If you need anything, just holler for Ruby. I'm surprised she didn't want to stay. I'm still so tickled that you two know each other. Small world, isn't it?"

Apparently far too small.

Elliot watched Connie put on her shoes and bustle out the door. He glanced at Grandma Lucy. Why was she staring at him like that? He could only meet her gaze for a few seconds.

He was being ridiculous. He'd never expected to see Ruby again after what happened between them, but that didn't mean he needed to act like some terrified little foster kid who refused to speak for days on end and could never maintain eye contact with anyone.

He looked at Grandma Lucy once more. "It's so nice of you to invite me to visit."

Why did she look so serious? It was almost as if she were angry at him. What had he done?

No, it wasn't anger. So why was she staring at him like that?

"You have a lovely house," he finally offered after a long silence. Why wouldn't she talk?

"It's very cozy." His voice trailed off.

Grandma Lucy shut her eyes. Had he seriously traveled over the North Cascades just to watch some old lady take a nap?

Apparently so.

He glanced at the staircase where Ruby had disappeared, his only solace knowing that she wasn't witnessing his floundering attempts to talk to this old woman.

He understood why Ruby left so suddenly. He'd seen the embarrassment in her eyes too.

Maybe that's why this conversation between him and Grandma Lucy got off to such an awkward start. Elliot wanted to start everything over, but how could he do that if the old woman was asleep?

He glanced at the clock, wondering if he should wake her up or let her have a little rest. It wasn't like he had anywhere else to go. But still, he hadn't come all this way to eat goat yogurt.

He cleared his throat, hoping to wake her up without sounding rude. Her eyes shot open and locked with his. "Prince of glory, Son of creation, firstborn from among the dead."

What was she saying?

"We thank you and praise you for this young man's life, his ministry, and his calling to be an agent of your comfort and healing."

Once Elliot figured out Grandma Lucy was praying instead of sleeping, he didn't know if that made his situation more or less awkward. Either way, it didn't matter, because the old woman was apparently determined to pray whether he was comfortable with the idea or not.

"Father God, only you know the sorrows that he's endured, but I sense he's a young man who has suffered his share of trials, who is carrying his load of burdens, who is longing to lay his fears and doubts at your feet but doesn't know how. I see a young man who believes in you but is insecure in his faith, just like the father in the Scriptures who cried out *Lord, I believe. Help my unbelief.* May you do unto my friend here what you did for that father so many years ago. May you grant him the healing that is his through the powerful and victorious name of Jesus. May he understand the joy that comes from worshiping the true and risen Savior, the great and glorious King."

She held his gaze the entire time, and Elliot felt as if she had been staring into his soul. He was well aware of the way certain charlatans would pose as psychics and make statements that were so general they were bound to be true for ninety-eight percent of the population, but he thought through what the old woman had said in her prayer. It wasn't all that specific, but his heart had been pounding the entire time. His spirit seemed to develop fingers that reached out to grasp and touch and hold onto the power and intensity that had filled the room while she prayed.

Elliot believed in God. It was his last foster father, a pastor, who sat him down just a few weeks before his high school graduation and led him to Christ. Since that day, Elliot had never doubted God's existence, but he'd certainly never experienced anything like this either. Grandma Lucy's words had awakened in his soul a longing he hadn't even known existed.

How could a woman this old possess such strength?

While his pulse pounded in his ears, Elliot watched her stern, regal face melt into a soft smile. "I'm so glad you stopped by to visit." Her voice, previously so intense Elliot felt like he was breathing in the power of God, was now as cracked and warbled as you would expect from someone her age.

Elliot was so surprised at the sudden change, he wasn't sure what to say.

"Does your visit have to do with what we prayed about in Seattle?" Grandma Lucy prompted.

He nodded. The day he had first met this little old granny was the same day he'd had to look at Charis and her husband and tell them it was time to make hospice arrangements.

There was nothing more Elliot or his team could do for the young mother who'd been entrusted into their care.

It wasn't the first time Elliot had to deliver devastating news, and in his line of work as an oncologist, it certainly wouldn't be his last. Over the years, he'd stood patiently by as some family members yelled at him, swore at him, called him a liar, while others remained stoic and expressionless. A few cried right then and there, but none of them reacted like Charis's husband.

Standing next to his wife, the young man held his toddler in his arms while their infant slept peacefully on the hospital bed, looked Elliot square in the eye and declared, "God isn't finished with Charis yet. There's no way he'll be taking her home now. He's going to heal her completely."

A few years earlier, Elliot had followed with interest the case of the little Robertson boy, a child with terminal cancer on the East Coast whose parents fought the state for the chance to deny chemotherapy and pursue homeopathic remedies for their son. Religious fanaticism had played a role in that instance as well. Elliot knew from experience that hope was an effective tool in the healing process, but it was no cure.

Just look at what had happened to his fiancée.

Still, his job was to guarantee that Charis remained as comfortable as possible in her last days on earth, not to babysit her family. Some of his colleagues would have let that husband of hers carry on with his misplaced expectations all the way up to the moment when the tech arrived to wheel Charis's body down to the morgue, but Elliot was more compassionate than that. What greater sickness is there than shattered hope? More than any other disease, it was the most poisonous cancer known to humankind.

But Charis's husband wouldn't be deterred, and Elliot was prudent enough to know when he'd said and done enough.

"God's going to pull her through this," the young man declared. "You just wait and see."

Half an hour later, Elliot had been finishing his fruit salad when some little white haired old lady sat down next to him in the hospital cafeteria and said, "You look so troubled that I knew God wanted me to come over and have a word with you. How can I pray for you today?"

He didn't give her details. Even if it weren't for confidentiality laws, Elliot would never feel comfortable discussing his patients' care with a stranger. He'd hardly told the woman anything, yet before he knew it, she had grabbed one of his hands with both of hers and was praying for God to miraculously heal the patient Elliot had never mentioned.

He couldn't have guessed how long the prayer lasted, but when she was done she stood up. "I have to go now. I have an appointment, but here's what I'm going to do. I'm going to write down your name, and I'm going to be praying for you and your patient every single day, and when God heals her, I want you to call me. I'm leaving you with my number so you can let me know when God responds."

Elliot's faith had been so small, he didn't even know what he'd done with her phone number. He came across it by accident two months after Charis rose from her sickbed and left the hospital with her husband and her daughters in their double stroller, the scarf wrapped around her bald head the only indication of the battle she'd fought.

Last week, after yet another round of tests proved Charis was in perfect health, Elliot found Grandma Lucy's phone number after getting his Tesla detailed. He felt stupid calling, but somehow he couldn't stop himself.

The next thing he knew, he was sitting at her dining room table, telling her what general details he could about Charis's miraculous healing.

It took twice as long to get through as it might have otherwise, thanks to Grandma Lucy's propensity to clasp her hands or throw her arms in the air and shout "hallelujah" or "praise the Lord" every two or three sentences. But finally the entire story came out, and Grandma Lucy stared at him with rapture in her eyes.

"Don't we serve an amazing Lord? And I'm convinced that this woman, whoever she is — God knows her name even if I don't — is going to do mighty things for the kingdom of heaven because you called her to good works and you will equip her with everything she needs for life and godliness. You have restored to her the joy of her salvation. You have pulled her out of the mire and given her a firm place to stand."

Elliot blinked, wishing his mind could keep up with how quickly Grandma Lucy could switch focus. One minute she was talking to him, and then, without changing her tone or giving any other indication, she was praying. She went on for a little while longer, asking God to bless the woman's family, her ministry, her church, and then she was talking to Elliot again as if she'd never taken that time off from their conversation.

"Now, that's fabulous news, and the Lord knows I rejoice to hear it, but that's not the only reason you drove all the way out here, is it?"

CHAPTER 11

"Come on," Ruby hissed impatiently into her cell phone. "Come on, Jessi. Pick up."

Technically, Jessi was working at the daycare right now, but that had never kept her from answering Ruby's calls in the past.

"Come *on*."

"What are you calling me for?" Jessi asked before shouting, "*Bowman! Stop trying to make your baby sister eat that Barbie doll leg. That's just wrong on so many levels.* So what do you want?" Her attention was back on the phone call.

Ruby wasn't sure how soundproof her room was. She couldn't hear Elliot downstairs, but was there any way he might hear her?

"You'll never guess who's in my dining room right now as we speak."

"What? You bought a home and furnished your own dining room and didn't tell me? *Hey, don't run with that lollipop in your mouth. Snack time's over anyway. No, don't hand it to me. Go put it in the trash where it belongs. No, I said trash, not toilet. Get over here."*

Ordinarily, Ruby would call back when Jessi wasn't quite so busy, but this couldn't wait.

"Listen," she snapped. "You remember that guy?" She lowered her voice even more. "My mom's oncologist?"

"Holy cow, are you talking about the cancer doctor from Seattle who …"

Ruby shushed her. Next thing you knew, half the kids in Orchard Grove would know about what passed between Ruby and Dr. Jameson. "Keep your voice down."

"What? Why? Is he listening in on this phone call? Bowman, if I have to tell you one more time to stop feeding your boogers to your sister, I'm going to put you in time out. I mean it."

"No," Ruby hissed. "He's downstairs in my dining room."

"You don't have a dining room."

"Where I work." Ruby was a perfect example of patience with Grandma Lucy and could certainly handle a daycare full of rowdy kids better than Jessi, but right now she needed her friend to keep up. "He's downstairs talking to Grandma Lucy."

"About what happened between you two? Holy cow, is he, like, doing that thing where you go into the little box and say *bless me, Father, for I have sinned* or whatever?"

"What? No. That's not … Grandma Lucy's not a priest. And she's not Catholic. It's just …"

"So why is he there then? *All right. If you two can't share that dolly nicely with each other, I'm going to cut her in half so you stop fighting. Would you like that? Then get along.* Sorry. What'd you say?"

"I don't know why he's here. They met in Seattle, she prayed for him …"

"She did what to him? *Bowman, keep your boogers in your own mouth. I mean, no, that's not what I mean. Don't put them in your mouth* or *anyone else's.* This job is so disgusting," she added in a whisper. "Now what were you saying about Dr. Hottie?"

Ruby rolled her eyes. "That's not his name."

"Of course it's not. But isn't that why you …"

"Will you shut up and listen? He's here, he's talking to Grandma Lucy right now as we speak, and I have no idea what I'm going to do."

"Well, what are they talking about?"

"How should I know?" If Jessi made Ruby any angrier, she'd start yelling into the phone which would ruin the whole point of coming upstairs for privacy in the first place.

"You mean he's been down there all this time and you haven't listened in on a word they've said?"

"No. I didn't want him to see me."

"So don't let him see you. But you can bet your cute leather jacket that if I were you, I'd be finding some hideout and listening to every single thing they talk about."

"Why?"

"Leverage. Or maybe just because I'd be dying of curiosity otherwise. Come on. Don't you want to know what Dr. Hottie drove all the way out from Seattle to get off his chest?"

"Will you stop calling him that?"

"Only if you tell me you were wrong and he's not hot at all."

Ruby rolled her eyes. "Yes, I was wrong. We all know how wrong I was. In fact, you were the first one to tell me just how wrong I was, and now you won't let me forget."

"So he's not hot. Then are you sure you weren't drunk that night, because I can't figure out why ..."

"Will you stop talking about that night and tell me what I should do now that he's here?"

"What are you talking about? *Girls, if I have to tell you to share that stupid, ugly doll one more time, I'm going to tie her from the ceiling and let Bowman hit her like a piñata until her head pops off. Got it?* You still there? Good. I already told you what you should do. Go listen in. Figure out why he's here. Then call me back in like half an hour because we're going to be doing that ridiculous YouTube little kiddie exercise thing, and I swear I'm going to lose my head if I have to hear those stupid songs one more time. *Bowman, what did I tell you about ...*"

The line went dead. Ruby stared at her phone.

Go listen in.

That was just like Jessi. No wonder she had gotten Ruby into so much trouble when they were teens.

Go listen in.

Well, it would beat sitting around here freaking out. Maybe Jessi had the right idea after all.

CHAPTER 12

Elliot didn't even know where to begin. All the questions he'd so methodically listed out on the drive over the North Cascades had melted into mush during Grandma Lucy's prayer session.

"I'm starting to wonder what you want me to say." Grandma Lucy folded her hands on her lap. Her placid smile bore no indication of the intensity that infused her voice and her presence any time she started to pray. "Do you want me to give you some magic cure that will heal all your patients at once? It doesn't work like that."

"I know it doesn't. I just wanted to know why it … how it …"

"Why God chose to heal this young mother you told me about while letting so many others die from their sickness?"

"Yeah." It sounded like such a stupid question when she put it like that though. Who was Elliot to question God's ways?

Grandma Lucy closed her eyes. Elliot suspected another

prayer was coming, but instead she just nodded her head, then looked at him again. "The Lord's ways certainly are mysterious, aren't they? Do you want to tell me what's really troubling you?"

He didn't come here to talk about Amy, but his story tumbled out nonetheless.

"I was engaged a few years ago. Amy and I met while I was in med school, and she was finishing her teaching degree. We were … She was perfect. Everything I could have wanted and then some."

What was he saying? It sounded like he was writing some cheesy Valentine's Day card. This wasn't going well.

"She loved kids. I mean, you'll never meet a teacher more devoted to her classroom. And she got involved in their day-to-day lives too. She'd bring extra food every single day because she had several kids who qualified for the school lunch program, but their parents never sent in their paperwork." Elliot didn't know why he was telling all this to a stranger. How long had it been since he talked about Amy to anybody?

"What happened to her?" Grandma Lucy asked the question with such certainty in her voice, Elliot wouldn't have been surprised if she started to recite the rest of their story for him.

"We got engaged. She wanted to wait until I was finished with med school, but then she got diagnosed with cancer." He shook his head, his entire body heavy with memories. "She promised me she'd get better. She'd sit in that hospital bed ear-marking pages in those wedding magazines, had the nurses tape pictures of some of her favorite gowns on the walls of her room. She told me when she got better we'd get married.

"I guess I was the more realistic one. Knew the course of the disease. Knew she wasn't doing well, but she had so much hope, and I just thought that maybe — just maybe — all those wedding pictures and our love for each other would be enough."

"But it wasn't." Grandma Lucy spoke softly. Elliot heard her but was too absorbed in his story to stop.

"I begged her to marry me. I told her we'd buy her the most beautiful wedding gown in any of those magazines, we'd get the nurses to help dress her up, and we'd bring in a chaplain or a preacher or somebody to do the ceremony for us, but she told me no. *No, we need to wait.* That's what she said. *I always dreamed of walking down the aisle, and that's what's going to happen.*"

He hadn't told this story in years. Memories that had once been drenched in sorrow now poured out in anger.

Anger at the cancer itself, at the doctors who failed to save her, at the God she'd so blindly trusted to heal her.

Anger at Amy for being so stubborn.

For deliberately deceiving him. All those wedding pictures, her talk of being healed, the whole time, she was lying.

"You know the real reason she didn't marry me? Her sister told me after the funeral. Amy knew she was going to die, and she didn't want me to take over all her medical bills when it happened. We could have ..." He sniffed. It was stupid to stay mad all these years, but he couldn't help it.

"You loved her deeply," Grandma Lucy replied.

Of course he had. Why else would he have proposed to her in the first place?

"And you're angry at the Lord for taking her away."

Well, what if he was? Who could blame him for that?

Grandma Lucy took his hand in hers, and before he could say or do anything, she was praying again.

CHAPTER 13

Great. Why had Ruby slipped the door open like that? Why had she snuck to the top of the staircase, like a little kid spying on their parents?

This wasn't her business. This tragic story about Dr. Jameson and his dead fiancée wasn't for her to know.

But now she did.

Which made her feel even more wretched about what had happened between them.

How many years ago had his fiancée died? Did he mention any dates? She tried to do the math. Was it anywhere close to the time when Ruby's mom had been one of his patients?

Her phone rang, and she sprang to her feet and raced back into her room.

"Hello?"

"Ruby. Where have you been? I thought I told you to call me. The kids are screaming for more of those YouTube kiddie exercise videos. I swear, those men who dress up in those costumes and get those stupid songs stuck in my head must be the most deranged people on the entire planet. Now I understand why the parents drop these brats off here, so we're the ones who have to suffer. I'm literally walking to the clinic after my shift's over and getting myself sterilized."

Ruby was hardly paying attention. There was never a day when Jessi didn't complain about her job at the daycare. It was a toss-up to decide which surprised Ruby more, why Jessi hadn't quit or why she hadn't already been fired.

"You two girls keep your hands to yourselves, or I swear I'm going to feed your fingers to my pet crocodile," she hollered. "Anyway, what's going on with Dr. Hottie?"

"Stop calling him that," Ruby huffed. "His name's Dr. Jameson."

"Fine. What's going on with Dr. Jameson? Is he still there? What's he wearing? Is he in casual? Please tell me he's in casual. I can just see him now. New jeans, kind of tight in the butt, one of those muscle men shirts showing off his arms ..."

"He's not that kind of guy."

"Well what kind of guy is he then?"

Couldn't Jessi do something helpful, like tell Ruby what to do with him in her house?

"He's just normal."

"Normal? Come on. That's not how things sounded when he was taking care of your mom."

"Will you leave my mom out of this?" Ruby hadn't meant to raise her voice. At least not that loud.

"Sheesh. I'm sorry. It's just that I happen to remember someone a few years ago telling me every single day how dreamy her mom's doctor was, how strong he looked … And then when you two …"

"Cut it out. I'm dead serious."

Jessi let out her breath. "Fine. You don't want to tell me what he looks like, doesn't matter to me. I'll just swing over there when I'm off work …"

"No, stay away." The last thing Ruby needed was Jessi here with him.

With Dr. Jameson.

No, Elliot.

It felt so strange to think of him like that. Like a person. A person who right now was downstairs chatting away with her patient.

Ruby's phone beeped. It was time for Grandma Lucy to take her medicine.

"Listen, I've got to go."

"You gonna head down there and talk to him?"

Ruby was appalled. "Of course not." The only question

was how to get Grandma Lucy her medicine without having to interact with Dr. Jameson — or Elliot — at all.

"I think you should. Walk right up to him and say, 'Hey remember me? You were the doctor who took care of my mom when she was …'"

"I told you to cut it out."

Jessi let out her breath. "Fine. I've got to go anyway. These kids are going to make me deaf in addition to driving me mad. You better promise to come visit me when I'm in my padded room and straightjacket, all from having to watch too many of these stupid YouTube videos."

Ruby was glad when the call ended, but her phone continued to beep. Grandma Lucy could go another five or ten minutes before she took more pills, but what if she and Elliot hung around all afternoon?

What if Connie convinced him to stay for dinner? She should call Jessi back right now and make plans to hang out tonight. She was about to start a text when Connie called up the stairs, "Ruby? Oh, Ru-by! I have some more snack things laid out, hon. Come help yourself. Ruby?"

She got herself out of the room before Connie had to come up the stairs and carry her down.

I'm a professional. I'm an adult. I can do this.

Ruby hadn't worked herself ragged through nursing

school just so she could stay up in someone's attic, hiding from awkward situations. Maybe Jessi was right. Instead of dying of humiliation every time she thought of Elliot Jameson, maybe it was time to confront him and get it over with.

Show him she wasn't the same person she'd been.

Show him she wasn't embarrassed about what happened.

Of course, she'd be lying through her teeth, but if Ruby had learned anything from her best friend, it was how to be dramatic.

CHAPTER 14

Elliot glanced at the time, calculating how soon he'd have to leave if he wanted to make it back to Seattle at a reasonable hour. He was still mad at himself for coming all the way out here. Grandma Lucy hadn't told him anything he didn't already know.

Some people God healed.

Some people he didn't.

And if Grandma Lucy couldn't explain how or why God chose to heal who he did, there wasn't a soul on earth who could.

It was even worse with Ruby here. When he first saw her, he thought for a split second it might work out best if they pretended to have never met, but there she had stood, smiling at him sarcastically.

Was she teasing him even now? Even after all these years?

Why had he come out to Orchard Grove? There was nothing for him in this town.

Absolutely nothing.

He cleared his throat. "Well, thank you so much for the visit. I'd better get back on the road soon."

Connie had recently come in from the gift shop and was bustling around the kitchen. "You can't leave yet. We're about to sit down for a snack, and I refuse to let you drive all the way back home hungry."

Elliot wondered if he should mention that he'd been eating ever since he arrived here.

"And I know for a fact there's no decent restaurants between here and Seattle," Connie was saying, "so I already decided we're gonna just have to keep you over for dinner. No use sending you all that way on an empty stomach. It's almost as dangerous as driving drunk, you know."

Elliot stood from the table. "No, really, I should be ..." He paused when he saw Ruby standing in the middle of the staircase. There she was with that ironic grin.

He recalled the day in fourth grade he'd stayed inside during recess in tears, sobbing about how much he hated being bullied. Mrs. Winifred had hugged him. She was one of the only teachers he remembered from his childhood who never shied away from physical contact with her students. She had hugged him and all but promised that things would get easier.

"When you're a smart, rich, successful adult, I guarantee you these meanies won't have anything bad to say to you ever again."

He'd believed Mrs. Winifred because he'd been so desperate for hope.

Turned out she was wrong.

Except now it wasn't stupid buck-toothed boys calling him Smelly Elly and making fun of him for being the only kid in class who couldn't run the hundred-meter dash without pulling out his inhaler.

Now it was Ruby, smiling at him so sarcastically.

She was gorgeous. That's what made it worse. And she knew it too, or she never would have pulled such an awful prank on him that night.

Dear God, please make her forget, he prayed, but the mischievous twinkle in her eye told him clearly she remembered every vivid detail.

All right, he shot back to the Lord. *If that's not going to work, you'll have to make me forget.*

He waited. Apparently God was out of miracles for the moment.

Connie smiled at Ruby. "Oh, good. You're here. Have a seat. I'm just getting ready to pull the muffins out of the oven."

"I need to go get Grandma Lucy's medicine." Ruby slipped down the hall. The smile was gone, and she didn't even acknowledge Elliot.

He was nothing to her, and she was going to remind him of that every second he stayed under this roof.

CHAPTER 15

Ruby locked herself in the bathroom and let out the breath she'd been holding. This was ridiculous. She was acting like a child. Her heart pounded wildly, and her hands had started to sweat.

Gross.

She opened the medicine cabinet, staring at her reflection in the mirror. It was no wonder Elliot didn't give her a second glance when she came downstairs. Her mouth was huge, her nose was way too pointy, her hair was tangled up in a messy bun, and she was ghastly pale. How long had it been since she went tanning? Sometime before she and Mace broke up.

She'd have to call Jessi and make appointments to get themselves some color again.

Ugh. Why did they even put mirrors in bathrooms?

She grabbed the prescription she was looking for and shut the cabinet. Her choices were to stay in here and stare at her too pale complexion and too bushy eyebrows or go out there and face Elliot.

She'd never once been accused of being a coward.

Today was no day to start acting like one

She squared her shoulders, set her jaw, and shut off the light, resisting the urge to glance in that mirror again.

Grandma Lucy was offering a blessing for the food. Ruby hung back in the hallway until she finished. It was nearly time for Grandma Lucy's afternoon nap. She'd be extra tired after praying with company for so long. It wasn't right for Elliot to come over here and ruin their entire schedule. Didn't he know her patient was sick?

Except Grandma Lucy was having one of her good days. Which meant she'd probably argue that she'd didn't need her medicine.

Ruby sat down next to her. "Here, Grandma Lucy. Time for your prescription." She was acutely aware of Elliot sitting there across the table watching her, judging her, but she had resolved not to care.

What happened between them was years in the past. Not worth worrying over or even remembering.

Grandma Lucy was surprisingly agreeable and easily swallowed the liquid in the syringe.

Ruby relaxed. No fights today. Maybe Grandma Lucy was too tired.

Connie was bustling around them with twice the energy of the rowdiest kids in Jessi's daycare. "It's so nice to have you stay with us for a spell, Elliot. You know, we don't have visitors as often now that Grandma Lucy's sick."

Ruby glanced at her patient. Usually even the suggestion that she wasn't in perfect health would get Grandma Lucy agitated, but she continued to smile pleasantly. Maybe Elliot was a good influence on her.

Or maybe he'd overstayed his welcome and she was simply exhausted.

Connie set some muffins and fruit and plenty of other items on the table. This was the second snack of the afternoon and was enough to feed a large family.

She stole a quick glance at Elliot, wondering where he grew up. Hadn't he gone to school somewhere out east? She thought she remembered seeing one of those Ivy League diplomas in his office back when he was taking care of her mom.

She clenched her muscles to ward off a shudder. As long as she didn't think about that office of his, she could make it through this afternoon. She turned to Grandma Lucy.

"Are you hungry? Can I get you something?"

The old woman was asleep in her chair.

Great.

Connie made comments while she continued laying things out on the table, and Ruby did her best to convince herself this wasn't the most painfully awkward encounter of her life. Stealing glances at Elliot, she wondered what she'd ever seen in him to begin with. He was tall and at least somewhat athletic-looking, not a bodybuilder or football star but with the physique of a runner. She watched him take a generous helping of fruit and avoid any of Connie's famous baked goods and wondered if he was some sort of health nut, the kind to wake up at five every morning for advanced yoga classes.

Not that she expected many medical residents had time to kill at the gym. It was hard to picture him as a doctor. He seemed so young, hardly older than she was. But now the difference between them in life experience could be measured in decades. Here he was with his MD, and what did she have except for a nursing license? Sure, she'd worked hard for that slip of paper, but he was so obviously out of her league it was embarrassing to imagine what he must think of her behavior.

Maybe she was being too hard on herself. She could blame that stupid night on the stress of watching her mom fighting off cancer, couldn't she? That had to count for something, didn't it?

Of course, he wouldn't see it that way. Not Mr. Ivy League Tan Skin Broad Shoulders …

Okay, so maybe she hadn't been totally honest when she told Jessi he wasn't good-looking. Maybe she simply wasn't thinking clearly since the moment he walked into Safe Anchorage.

Wasn't Grandma Lucy supposed to be super connected to God? Couldn't the Lord have told her what a terrible idea this meeting would be?

And now she was asleep, leaving Ruby to stare or not stare at Elliot while Connie ran around like a chicken with its head cut off — an idiom Ruby never fully understood before living at Safe Anchorage Farms.

"So tell me," Connie began, setting glasses of lemonade on the table.

Ruby wanted to disappear, certain she knew what Connie was going to ask next.

"I think it's so fascinating that you two already know each other. How did you meet?"

CHAPTER 16

Ruby stared at Connie.

Then at Elliot.

"We were at …"

"I was working …"

They both paused.

Connie stopped her scurrying and stared at them both.

Ruby took a deep breath. "Dr. Jameson was one of my mom's doctors."

"I was just starting my residency," Elliot explained. He looked down, and for a second Ruby got the nagging suspicion that he was just as uncomfortable as she was.

"And now here you both are in Orchard Grove of all places." Connie clasped her hands together. "Isn't that something?"

The landline phone on the wall rang. Connie glanced at it. "I'm sorry, children. That's the gift shop calling. I better see what they need."

She picked up the receiver and talked for just a moment,

concluding with the ominous, "I'll be right over."

Ruby was tempted to pinch Grandma Lucy in the side to wake her.

Connie hung up the phone. "There's a problem with the credit card machine again. I declare, this newfangled technology …" She hurried to put on her shoes. "I won't be but a minute." And she was out the door.

Great.

Ruby glanced at Elliot.

He looked at a point past her shoulder.

What now?

"So you've finished nursing school?" he finally asked.

She nodded. She'd been so young back when they first ran into each other.

Young and stupid. And he was going to remind her of that with every single thing he said.

The jerk.

"Have you been doing home care for a while now?"

She shook her head. "I was at the local hospital here at first. Just started working for Grandma Lucy a little bit ago."

If she didn't know better, she would have said he cracked a smile. The nerve. As if he knew how embarrassed she was, but he just kept talking.

"Which do you like better? Hospital or home?"

What a stupid question. If she preferred the hospital environment, wouldn't she have stayed there? Next thing you knew, he was going to ask how many other doctors she'd cornered into back rooms and made out with while her mom was fighting for her life the next room over.

Nope. She didn't have to sit here and take this. She stood up and cleared her throat. "Well, it's great to see you again," she began sarcastically, but he stopped her.

"Wait. I need to go soon too, but I wanted to ask you something."

She paused with her hand on the back of her chair. "What?" This was good. As long as she could feel angry at him instead of humiliated, she could make it through one or two more minutes of torture.

"I wanted to ask about your mom. I never heard."

"She died."

He lowered his eyes. "Oh. I'm sorry." At least he had the decency to sound sincere.

She shrugged. "It was a long time ago."

He was standing now too. "I wish …" He cleared his throat before trying again. "I wish you all the best. And that's really too bad about your mom. She was a strong woman."

Ruby gave her head a slight tilt. "Yes, she was."

Just not strong enough to beat the cancer.

"I think I'd better go," he said. "I'll stop by and say goodbye to Connie at the gift shop. It's just that building across the driveway, isn't it?"

Ruby nodded.

"Well ..." He looked around as if there were anything left to say. "I guess Grandma Lucy's asleep, isn't she?"

Wow. For a med school graduate, wasn't he Mr. Observant? Ruby didn't bother with a response.

Elliot paused for another second, gave her a curt nod, and walked out the front door.

Ruby sank back into her chair. He was gone.

And not a moment too soon.

CHAPTER 17

Once Elliot stepped into the gift shop, he had to muster every ounce of his self-control and social etiquette not to step back out immediately. For an asthmatic with sensitivity to heavy perfumes, the entire building was a nightmare.

He saw Connie behind the counter and waved. "Just wanted to let you know I'm taking off."

She hurried toward him. He kept the door propped open with his foot, his promise to his lungs that he'd be out in the fresh air soon.

"You sure you can't stay with us for dinner? Grandma Lucy will be so disappointed."

He shook his head. "It'll be late by the time I get home, and I've got work tomorrow."

She let out a dramatic sigh. "Well, I'm mighty glad you stopped by for a visit. And I do hope you come again. Especially since you and Ruby go way back. You know, I've been praying for God to send her some nice, respectable friends. You should see the crowd she used to hang out with.

Now, I know it's not my business what she does when she's off the clock, but it sure would be a welcome change to have some young folks like you stopping by the house who know their manners and treat Grandma Lucy nice."

Elliot's breath was so short, he had to leave. "I'm sorry to be rude, but I really have to go." He coughed. "It's … it's …" He waved his hand in front of him and stepped back outside.

Air.

The bells on the store door jingled when Connie followed him out. "Everything all right, hon?"

"Yeah." He took in another breath. "I'm just a little asthmatic, and the perfumes …"

She frowned. "I should have warned you about that. Those come from all our goat-milk lotions and candles and things. I'm so sorry if it was bothersome for you. Can I get you something? Some lemonade? Maybe a cinnamon roll or two?"

He couldn't help but smile. "No, I'm fine." Amazing what a little fresh air could do.

"Well, you take care now." Connie reached out and wrapped him in a hug as if she were saying goodbye to her long-lost child. "We're sure going to miss you. And you better believe that Grandma Lucy will be praying for you and all your patients."

"Thanks."

Glad that he didn't have to extend his stay in Orchard Grove a minute longer, Elliot made his way to his Tesla.

It was time to go home.

CHAPTER 18

Mace

I've got my little sister yakking in one ear, and I'm listening to the curses of all the video-game aliens I'm blowing up in the other.

"Uh-huh," I say, because even though I'm paying more attention to my first-person shooter than I am to my sis, I've learned that all Jessi really needs is someone to complain to about her work at that nasty, germ-infested daycare.

It's not like I need to actually pay attention.

Blue guts spray onto my screen, and I literally lean my whole body to the side like I'm about to dodge them. It's not 3D, but the graphics on this thing are just as good as the reviews said they'd be.

"So then, I told those two little brats that if they couldn't agree to take turns with that stupid, ratty doll ..."

"Uh-huh," I say and kill two more aliens that look quite a bit like lizards.

"Are you even listening to me?" she snaps.

"Uh-huh." I rewind the conversation in my brain. I can do that, you know. Comes in extremely handy when I'm talking to my sis. "You were telling me about the boy who kept trying to feed boogers to his little brother."

"It was his little sister," she corrects, and I wonder why I never tried that booger trick when I was that kid's age. Or maybe I did. Not like I can remember that far back.

"Anyway, that's not what I was saying," Jessi continues, and I don't really want to get into a fight, but I know she's wrong, so I give her the typical "nuh-uh," we've been using since we were as young as the monsters she has to watch. It's a terrible job, but she's got to pay the rent somehow.

I told her that she and Ruby may as well live together. It'd save my sis a ton of money having one more roommate, and she and Ruby have been best friends for as long as I can remember and then some, so I have no idea why they both think it's such a terrible idea.

Must be a girl thing.

I've got to be careful because I know those stupid aliens have booby-trapped this whole blasted building. One wrong step, and I'll be the one splattering my guts on the screen.

"Are you playing that dumb game of yours?" Jessi demands, and she's not here to see me roll my eyes.

"I'm listening," I tell her, just barely missing a tripwire that would've blown my leg off for sure.

Tricky aliens.

"Did you hear what I said about Ruby?"

"Huh? What?" I rewind in my head, but I'm certain I would have paid attention if Jessi had mentioned my girlfriend.

Or ex-girlfriend.

At least she is now, but not for long.

I think this is our sixth or seventh breakup. It's probably more if you count junior high, but seriously, who counts junior high?

The longest we've been broken up is five months, and if I'm doing the math in my head right, we've been separated for about three this go-around already, so it can't be too much longer.

Jessi's got this whiny tone in her voice. It's no wonder she hasn't found herself a boyfriend yet. "I said that some dude from Seattle came to visit Ruby's patient at the farm today."

"Uh-huh." There's a huge explosion ahead of me, and the skinny chick in leather who's supposed to be my guide is lying in a pool of blood.

Oops.

"Are you listening?" Jessi snaps.

Great. I've got five of these lizard dudes coming up on me at once, and that leather chick who was supposed to show me the way out of here is dead.

Should have saved the game before I went through that door.

"Uh-huh," I tell my kid sis. "The old lady's got some Seattle city boy coming to the farm. So?"

"So, Ruby knows him."

"Uh-huh." I'm trying to remember the way out of here, but I've only gotten this far once before. Come to think of it, Jessi was yakking into my one ear that afternoon too, telling me I need to get off my butt and ask Ruby out again.

Because we all know that's my next move. I've just been a little busier than normal since they came out with the third Alien Slayers. That's all.

"Will you turn that stupid game off and listen to me?"

"Yeah, sure," I say and hit mute. With my guide dead, it's not like I'll miss anything on mute except for all these aliens screaming at me. Dang. One clawed my leg. My health is down to ten percent.

"It's not really off, is it?" Jessi complains, and I don't know if it's because she's distracting me or if the aliens really are that good, but one of them takes a lunge and must have gotten me right in the neck because there's a spurt of blood, and then I'm dead.

I pause before the game automatically reloads. Time to get me something to eat anyway.

"It's off now," I tell her. "What do you want?"

She sighs, and I can tell by the impatient *it's about time* sound that she believes me. "So this Seattle guy came to visit Ruby …"

"You told me he came to visit that crazy old lady." See? I'm better at listening to my sister than she is at hearing herself.

"It's not like that."

"Like what?" I open up the freezer and pull out some frozen pepperoni pizzas. My electric was out for a few days, so I hope it hasn't gone bad.

"Yes, he came to visit the old lady," my sis says like she thinks I'm as stupid and dense as those brats she watches all day, "but he knows Ruby from way back."

I lean down by the fridge and pull out a Mountain Dew. Have I had anything to drink today? I can't remember.

I pop the can open. Don't you love the sound of soda fizz?

"Okay," I say after I take a big drink. "So what?"

"Are you dense? You've got competition now."

I nearly spray the Mountain Dew out my nose. "Say what?"

"Competition. I know it's a big word, but try to follow. It means there's someone else that Ruby …"

"Shut up," I say before my own kid sister starts to give me English lessons. "I know what the word means. But what makes you think it's got anything to do with me?"

Jessi's sigh is all annoyed and impatient. Like she can't believe she's stuck with a brother as stupid as me. Well, I've got news for her. I may be a sixth-year senior, and she might be Miss Associates Degree, but you don't see me wiping snotty noses and dirty butts all day, do you?

You want to tell me who's got the real brains in this family?

"Ruby had a thing with him," she tells me, and now I'm paying attention.

"What kind of a thing?" I ask, because with girls like my sister you never know. Is she talking about a thing? Or is she talking about a *Thing*?

"How many kinds of things are there?" she practically explodes all over me, and if she doesn't know the difference between a thing and a *Thing*, it's not worth my time trying to explain.

Jessi huffs again. I swear she sounds like she's just run a

mile the way she lets out her breath like that.

"Just hurry up, and do whatever you're gonna do," she tells me all bossy, "because this could get serious."

My ears are tingling. "How serious?" I stare at my Mountain Dew. It's probably my first drop of anything since last night before I went to bed, and I'm not even thirsty anymore.

"Just do something quick," Jessi tells me and hangs up.

CHAPTER 19

I may not have my college degree just yet, but I can recognize a good thing when it comes my way. You don't even want to know how far me and Ruby go back.

We met because she's my sister's best friend, but me and Ruby have always had something between us, even when she was a little scrawny six-year-old with her big nose and big ears and long limbs looking all awkward.

That girl could boss me around like nothing else. Make me put on a Burger King crown and pretend to be king, and that left Jessi to be the princess. Because both Jessi and me said it wouldn't work out for a brother and sister to be married, even in make-believe.

Same thing when those girls wanted me to play house. They had to bribe me. Ruby would bring over candy. Her mom kept her place loaded, and I'd have to make-believe with them for five minutes for every piece of candy they shared.

And since me and my sister couldn't be the parents, that

left me and Ruby getting ourselves married each and every time.

She was my first kiss. And I'm not talking about that time when I was nine and my sister dared me to. That was just one of those little kid pecks on the lips and didn't really count for anything worth mentioning.

We were only in junior high, but you know how kids are that age. Think they're mini adults. It was the Valentine's Day dance, or maybe the Christmas one. Ruby'd be mad if she knew I forgot, but what I didn't forget is the way we snuck out by the science lab and she pulled me by my hand and told me she had a secret to tell me, and then before I knew what was happening, my eyes were closed and her mouth was right there, and we just went right on kissing straight through the slow dance that was playing in the gym.

And finally when we were done, she said, "Think we'll always be this much in love?" and I said, "Uh-huh," like the fool I was because I had no idea how much more in love we'd get once we finally hit our growth spurts.

Sure, we fought all the time, but that's because we were as much brother and sister as we were boyfriend and girlfriend, and I guess the way I said that makes it sound pretty gross, but I don't mean it in any disgusting way. We'd grown up together and knew the best way to get on each other's nerves.

There was the time she accused me of cheating. And I don't mean cheating with another girl, I mean cheating like what you do when you steal someone's answers on a test. She knew I was bad at math, so she agreed to help me study, and when she finally realized all I wanted was for her to just go ahead and give me the right answers for my homework, she was pretty ticked.

We broke up around tenth grade because she got herself grounded, and I wanted her to sneak out anyway, but she wouldn't. It was a big bluff, though, and she knew it. Two weeks later when she finished her punishment, we were back together again.

It was right after I graduated high school that was the worst. I'm a year older than her and Jessi, so I went away to Spokane my first year. She sobbed and cried and swore I'd find me some college girl and forget all about her, and I cried and swore that'd never happen, but it did.

Just five months later I came around. Apologized over Christmas break, and Ruby was ready to forgive even if she didn't quite forget. We've been together ever since, except for the other smaller breakups, but most of those hardly lasted a few days.

Which is why the past few months have been so strange.

Ruby, she'd been working at the hospital, and one night she told me this granny lady fell and hit her head and needed Ruby to stitch her up.

Don't ask me what happened next because even though she's told me the story half a dozen times or more, I can never quite get over my shock. Ruby decided to become one of those Jesus people. You know who I mean. The ones who knock on your door handing out slips of paper that tell you what you have to do if you want to make your way to heaven. The ones who are all about keeping these strict rules, like always go to church on Sundays and never sleep with someone before you're married to them.

I'll admit that part was a little hard for me to accept. But we were practically engaged by that point anyway, so I just figured I could hold out a few months while we made the wedding plans.

Well, that's what was supposed to happen at least.

She thought I'd be mad at her. She was actually nervous telling me about her come-to-Jesus moment, truth be told. She thought I'd make a bigger deal about the whole sex before marriage thing too. I mean, if she'd come and told me she was going to stay a celebrity or whatever that word is where you never sleep with anybody for your entire life, well then I may have had a harder time, but like I said, I did the math and figured worse case was we'd have to wait a couple weeks. I mean, how long does it really take to buy a ring and plan a wedding, right?

So life was good. Sure, it was a little weird having her stop wanting to stay out late on Saturday so she could be to church on time and stuff the next day, but she's always put up with all my little quirks. I mean, how fun can it be for her to sit around and watch me play twenty hours of video games straight every time a new Alien Slayer comes out?

So I figured it was time for me to make a few compromises for her or however you want to say it.

No big deal.

Well, then she started hanging out with that Grandma Lucy lady even more. She's the one I told you about who hit her forehead and needed those stitches, and that's how she got to the point where she could introduce Ruby to Jesus to begin with, and now all of a sudden Grandma Lucy started taking this huge interest in her little student, and Ruby came home from one of their meetings telling me she was going to have to pray about whether or not we needed to break up.

"Why?" I asked, and I even paused my game right then because I got a feeling this was serious.

Well, Ruby said that Grandma Lucy was telling her how Christians shouldn't ever marry non-Christians, and how would we raise our children, and I was still thinking, *we're way too young to have kids anyway, so what's the big deal?* But Ruby was all upset, and that's when I realized she was seriously considering breaking up with me just because I don't wear a cross around my neck or go to church on Sundays. I told her, "You know what? I'm going to go ahead and save you the time. You don't have to pray about whether or not you're gonna break up with me because I've decided I don't want to be with a Christian anyway, not if it means you making me feel bad because I'm not just like you."

And she said, "When did I ever make you feel bad?" and honestly, I didn't have much to say. You know how some Christians get all stuffy and preachy? Ruby never got that way, but I figured it was only a matter of time before she turned into one like all the rest. So that's how we broke up most recently.

I was pretty upset too. Guess it makes sense. Not too many dudes my age have only been with one girl since junior high. I mean, if I was even willing to go however long without sleeping together just to make her conscience clean, you can tell how much she means to me. But apparently it wasn't enough, and sometimes I have a hard time knowing if I'm more angry at Ruby or at that Grandma Lucy lady who took her away from me in the first place.

And now my sister's warning me that there's some other dude hanging around and that he and Ruby had a *Thing* in the past, so I've got to make up my mind.

Do I run after her now and hope she's come to her senses and wants to be with me because of me — not because of what I do or don't believe in?

Or do I let her have her stuffy little Seattle guy, count my losses, and move on?

I stare at my Mountain Dew. I have a lot of thinking to do, don't I?

CHAPTER 20

Turns out it was an easier decision than I thought it would be. Forty minutes later, after I've eaten the last of the pepperoni pizzas, I'm at my friend's dorm bumming some gas money off him.

Time to head back to Orchard Grove.

I kind of hate that town. You know those Christians I mentioned earlier, the ones who you know are judging you no matter what you say or do?

Orchard Grove's full of them. My dad and I never agreed on much except being grateful we weren't like those churchy folks.

And now I'm driving over a hundred miles because I'm going to try to convince my ex-girlfriend, who now is one of those churchy folks herself, to take me back. I've even got the ring in my pocket. I found the right one three days before we broke up. Did I tell you that already?

I hope I'm not too late.

So she's got some other dude interested in her? I can

handle that. I'm not even the least bit intimidated. Know why? I've got history on my side. This other guy, he ain't got nothing on me.

And this sweat on my palms? That's just the caffeine. I knew it'd be a long drive, so I got myself a Rockstar on top of the Mountain Dew I had at the house, so yeah. None of this means I'm nervous.

Why would I be nervous? I don't have anything to worry about. And seriously. You should meet my sister. Can someone say drama queen? The *Thing* she says Ruby and this Seattle dude had? It could be as simple as he was the delivery man who dropped off her mail one day. That's literally all it might be, and Jessi would freak out about it.

That's just my sis.

So I'm not worried. Not about him.

What gets me going, even if it's just a little bit, is the whole church thing. Because seriously. Who can compete with God? I'm not afraid of Ruby picking Seattle Guy over me. I'm afraid she'll pick Jesus.

And then I don't know what I'd do.

Some people would tell me to go ahead and go to church with her. Become a member, all that stuff. Although I don't even know what you have to do to go about becoming a member at a church. Don't you have to promise them half of all your income or something? Oh well. The church can't take what I haven't earned.

Once I graduate and get myself a job that might turn into a thing. But not with a capital T at least.

So there's that option. Of course, if Ruby says she'll have me and I don't need to change at all — and that's what I'm hoping for — I don't have to even be thinking this through right now. But if she makes the church thing a deal-breaker, I could always go along with it.

Not like I'd be the first man who pretended to be all religious and spiritual just to make his woman happy, right?

But then I think about all those stuffy Christians I know, especially the ones at Orchard Grove Bible. You do not want to meet this crowd. There's a newer church somewhere in town. I suppose I'd be all right if Ruby wanted to go there, but I have the feeling she'll stick with that Bible Church since that's where her precious Grandma Lucy goes.

But see, I'm not even sure how I feel about going along with faith just to get the girl. It might not be an outright lie, but it'd be pretty close to it. And the whole having kids thing … I know neither Ruby or me are ready for that kind of responsibility yet. What would we do? All live together at that little farm house while Ruby works taking care of that old lady?

I'm in no rush to become a father tomorrow, but if Ruby and me get married, chances are we'll have a baby or two eventually. And then what? Do I just become the kind of dad who goes to church and says his bedtime prayers with his kids but doesn't believe it? I'm just not sure how good I'd feel about that.

And what if Ruby knows I'm a fake? What's that going to do to us?

So you can see I have a lot of things to decide. It's a good thing it's such a long drive back to Orchard Grove.

I just hope by the time I get there I've made up my mind.

This could turn into a very long night.

CHAPTER 21

"You there, Mace?" Jessi yells in my ear. I don't have my headset, so I have to put her on speaker. I might be a sixth-year senior, but that doesn't mean I'm an unsafe driver.

"Yeah. What you want?"

"I wasn't sure you'd really do it."

"Really do what? Drive out to Orchard Grove? Course I would."

My kid sister knows me better than that.

"You got the ring?"

"Course I do." Does she think I'd forget something that huge?

"You gonna give it to her?"

That's the question of the day, isn't it? "I'll see when I get there."

"What are you gonna say to her?"

In high school, Jessi hated me and Ruby being together. She was jealous of how much time I was spending with her best friend. But then when we all got older, it turned into this big deal, so every time Ruby and me broke up, Jessi would come over and practically try to beat me up she was so upset.

"Just hang up, and give me time to think," I say. I've only got an hour left in the car. I've been playing Alien Slayer so much this week I swear I'm seeing lizard monsters on the road in front of me. And where's the girl in leather who's supposed to be my guide?

I'm speeding, but who cares? There aren't any cops out this late, at least there never have been any of the other hundreds of times I made this trip.

It feels like I drive back to Orchard Grove every other week. Even when I'm not dating Ruby, my little sis always has something she wants me to do. And I'd never say it to her face, but I get so nervous when she heads out my way (see her behind the wheel, and you'd totally understand) that I try to be the one driving out to her instead of the other way around.

My stomach feels like it's tied up in knots, and I'm pretty sure it's not from the pizzas.

So why am I so nervous?

It might sound weird, but I literally can't remember a time I've been scared around Ruby. Mad as one of those lizard monsters in Alien Slayer? Yup. Or so sad when we break up that I'm nearly the drama queen my little sis is?

Done that too.

But afraid?

This is new.

You have no idea how much I wish that my only competition was the guy from Seattle.

I know I'd have a lot better luck against him than against a God you can't even see.

CHAPTER 22

"All right." Jessi's yakking on speaker phone. I'd never tell her, but at this point I've been on the road so long I'm glad for the company, even if it's just her voice. "So you're totally gonna apologize, right?"

"What do I have to apologize for?" I ask. Far as I remember, it was Ruby who threatened to leave me. I tell my sister so, and she practically jumps down my throat.

"You are such an idiot. I can't believe we're even related. You're the one who broke up with her, moron. And don't tell me it wasn't like that, because I've heard the story now from her side and yours, and that's one thing you both agree on."

"So?"

"So?" She's practically screaming now. I grin as I turn the volume down on my phone. Why can't I do that to her when we're together in person?

"Yeah," I repeat. "So?"

"So you've got to get on your knees and give her the most gorgeous, flowery, heart-felt apology of your life and beg her to make you her husband. Because as far as I see it, that's the only way she's gonna agree to anything."

"What about the whole Jesus thing?" I'm not sure Jessi's thought through this as much as she thinks she has. She may have graduated with an associate's degree and all, but that still doesn't make her a genius.

"You tell her that you're so happy she's found something that gives her life purpose and meaning. Because you and I both know she's always been a little off since her mom died. You tell her that you're gonna support her in her new faith, and if she asks about babies, you're gonna make sure she knows that you're totally fine having a whole bunch of little Christian kids running around and going to Sunday school and those funny church day camps they do every summer and anything else she tells you to do."

"What if I don't mean it?"

"You're serious?" Jessi sounds almost as mad as if I were one of the brats she takes care of at that daycare. "You're seriously going to turn that into an issue? You and I both know Ruby's the best thing that's ever happened to you besides the day I was born, and if you mess this up, there's a very decent chance I'll never forgive you. Not in a hundred years."

She sounds so whiney. Sometimes I forget we're both

adults now and not two little kids fighting over whose turn it is to play on the Nintendo.

"This isn't about you," I muttered. I don't think the speaker phone will pick it up, but it does.

"Of course this is about me. The day you fell in love with my best friend, it became about me."

How long ago was that, I wonder? When she was in first grade?

"Listen," I tell her, "I've got to go. Reception's not that great. You're cutting in and out."

"You're such a liar. I can't believe …" she starts and then I hang up.

CHAPTER 23

I text my little sis when I'm at the stop sign on Main Street and tell her I'm about five minutes away. It's late, but I don't think I've gone to sleep before 2 a.m. all semester, so I'm not worried. Besides, I picked up another energy drink at the gas station as soon as I landed in Orchard Grove, so it's not like I'd be hitting the pillow any time soon no matter where I was.

The last time I came here, I didn't see Ruby once. It was weird. I'm still trying to wrap my mind around being broken up.

Like the other night I was trying to beat this one level on a new console game I bought. It's this high fantasy thing, not my typical choice, but my electricity was still off so I had to come up with something I could do on my laptop, and this was the one I decided was least likely to drain my battery totally dry.

So I was at this kind of boring part, you know where you're not to the boss yet but you've racked up enough strength points that the fighting's pretty simple. To be honest, it was a pretty dumb quest to begin with, but that's how I feel about most console games anyway.

But the point is I wanted to call her, just to have someone to talk to. I mean, how exciting can it be when all you're doing is digging a hole and looking for a box that may or may not be buried there?

Ruby and me have been broken up for months, and I still can't get used to not talking to her whenever I want.

I'm getting closer to my sister's place now, and if I know Jessi, Ruby's gonna be there too. Except chances are Ruby'll have no idea I'm about to show up, so I need to come up with some plan. A script, know what I mean?

If she's happy to see me, that's going to make my work a whole lot easier for me.

And if she's not, I'll need to jump fast into that apology I've been working on ever since I hung up on my little sis.

Jessi may not be the brains in the family, but she knows Ruby. And I think she's right.

I've got to give her this apology, and I've got to make it good.

Problem is I pull up to Jessi's apartment, and Ruby's car isn't there. I'm not too worried. Maybe Jessi picked her up or something, brought her over here. For all I know, those

Christian wackos she lives with keep her locked up in a tower, and she has to sneak out every time she wants to have a little fun.

Not that I know what kind of fun Ruby can be having now that she's saved, but she's a smart girl. She'll have figured something out by now.

I hate to admit it, but when she first told me about this whole thing with Grandma Lucy and God, I thought it was a phase. I guess part of me still thinks it is, even though it's been going on a lot longer than I'd hoped. I expected a week or two tops. Once she realized that Jesus didn't have anything to offer but a lot of stuffy rules to follow, she'd be back to her fun-loving self again.

I guess I haven't completely tossed that idea away, but I'm starting to have my doubts.

I want to be mad at Ruby. I really do. We had this perfect plan. We were going to get engaged after I finished college (sixth year's a charm), we'd get married about a year later, and we still hadn't decided if we wanted to move to Spokane or Wenatchee, but we were definitely staying out of Orchard Grove and settling down in a real city. Ruby could find work as a nurse anywhere. Literally. Have you heard the statistics? There isn't a single hospital in Washington state that isn't hiring nurses.

Or at least something like that.

I figured we had the perfect plan. Nobody said it, but it was sort of understood Jessi would move out wherever we were. I mean, if you think Ruby and me were close, it's nothing compared to what those two got. They literally can't spend more than two or three days without seeing each other, giggling and gossiping or whatever it is girls their age do when they get together. Maybe they wax their legs or something. How in the world should I know?

But then Ruby went and changed everything up. First is the whole Jesus thing, then her crazy old lady patient tells her we shouldn't be dating since I'm not a believer.

As if that means anything.

I believe in lots of things.

Doesn't everybody?

What she should say is that I'm not a believer in the exact same things she is. You've got to spell it all out when you're putting labels on people. And if you want my opinion, this world has too many labels as it is.

I walk into Jessi's apartment, and there's my little sis on the couch eating ice cream.

"Hey, Jelly," I say because I've never called her anything else in my entire life, at least not that I can remember. I was only a toddler when she was born, and I suppose it's the best

I could do. The name stuck for years, but now I'm the only one in the family to still use it.

Jessi's up hugging me and yelling at me at the same time, wondering what took me so long, telling me I should have texted when I was close so she'd be ready.

"I texted you at the stop sign," I say, and she looks around the room all lost.

"Oh. I guess my phone was in the bedroom."

I roll my eyes, then pick her up like I always do when we haven't seen each other in a while.

"Haha, very impressive. Yes, you're very strong," she tells me.

I set her down.

"Where's Ruby?"

"Who?"

I don't want to play guessing games so I just stare.

Jessi shrugs. "I suppose she's at that farmhouse of hers."

"Didn't you tell her I was coming?" I ask.

"Of course I didn't. She'd never stop by if she knew I was trying to set the two of you up again. In fact, she made me promise to drop it the last time I tried. You want to talk to her, you're gonna have to find her."

This wasn't like my little sis. "Wait, I drove all the way out here …"

"To watch me eat ice cream?" Jessi raises her eyebrows.

"Where's Ruby?" I feel like I'm stuck in some sort of sci-fi time loop, starting the same conversation we just finished.

"Probably with her farm people."

"You should have called her over." Am I repeating myself? Maybe. But it's Jessi's fault. Does she think I can just stay up all night driving over the entire state?

"I did," Jessi huffs, and now some of the mystery is starting to make more sense.

"I called her and asked her if she wanted to come over for some chick flicks, but she said she was tired and wanted to go to bed early."

"How long ago was that?" I ask. I'm panicked now.

Jessi looks at her clock. "About two hours."

Great. I don't bother to hug her goodbye because no matter how the rest of tonight goes, we both know I'll stop by here and see her again. What day is tomorrow? I can't even remember what time I've got to get to class.

Well, all that can wait. I'm about to go find Ruby.

This ring is burning a hole in my pocket.

CHAPTER 24

"Grandma Lucy asleep?" Connie asked after she came in from tucking the goats into the barn for the night.

Ruby set down her mug of tea and nodded. She was so tired. Jessi had asked her over for a movie night, and Ruby had turned her down so she could drink tea and go to bed early.

What was happening to her?

Connie washed her hands at the sink, then started wiping down the counters, which were spotless as always. "Well, thanks again for your help with Grandma Lucy. She had a real good afternoon, didn't she?"

Ruby nodded. On days like this, she felt guilty to be employed here. Connie and her husband certainly weren't rich. They had the goat business and the gift shop, but Ruby guessed it was still a strain to be paying her to take care of an old woman who half the time didn't need her at all. Hopefully insurance would start covering things before long, and Ruby wouldn't feel so bad.

She finished off her tea. If she didn't hurry, Connie would sit down and then another hour or two could pass before bed. It wasn't that late yet. Maybe she'd text Jessi and let her know she'd changed her mind.

Connie pulled out some bread rolls. That was Ruby's cue to leave. If she ate every single pastry Connie laid out for her, she'd gain a pants size a month.

Ruby let out her breath. "Well, I guess I'll head upstairs."

"You don't want a snack?"

Ruby didn't look at Connie's expression. She didn't want to feel even guiltier.

"No, I'm pretty tired. It's been a long day."

CHAPTER 25

Back home. Finally. Elliot turned on the lights in his studio apartment. It wasn't the nicest place to live, but it was close to the hospital, and with as much as he was paying to drive that Tesla of his, he couldn't afford any superfluous expense.

He tossed the keys onto the counter. What a day.

He wasn't hungry, but he opened his fridge automatically. He was about to grab some yogurt but then remembered how much he'd eaten at Grandma Lucy's house. Better not overdo it on the dairy.

Settling on some carrot sticks and hummus, he plugged his cell phone in to charge, then stared at it longer than he should have.

Was he seriously thinking of calling her?

Ruby. She'd been so young when they first met. Still in nursing school. Her mom had boasted about what a hard worker she was, how she took a full course schedule and worked part-time to offset costs.

Ruby's mom had been one of Elliot's youngest patients. He would never forget her even if it hadn't been for her daughter.

He understood why Ruby acted the way she did, even more so now that he'd been in the field for a few years. He'd seen family members behave in bizarre ways while they tried to cope with the pain of watching their loved ones suffer.

It had been a vulnerable time for Elliot too.

Which is why he was thinking of calling. To apologize.

He had the Safe Anchorage house number in his phone. All it would take was one little button.

But it was late. Maybe he should wait. Then again, tomorrow he'd be working another eighteen-hour shift.

He sighed. It had to be now. He hadn't even touched his hummus.

His hands were steady when he picked up his cell.

"Hello, Connie?" he said. "I hope I didn't wake you. It's Elliot. I was wondering if Ruby was free to talk?"

CHAPTER 26

Someone was on the phone for her? And calling the house?

This was new.

Connie handed Ruby the receiver.

"Hello?"

"Ruby? It's me. Dr. Jameson." He lowered his voice. "I mean Elliot."

Great. What did he want? "Yeah?"

She hoped he was calling just to let her know he'd left his driver's license or something and needed her to stick it in tomorrow's mail. But then why couldn't he have asked Connie?

There was an awkward pause. "Are you busy? I wanted to talk to you about something."

Connie continued to stare at her. Ruby took in her breath, trying to steady her voice. "Yeah. Can you call my cell?"

"Sure." He sounded relieved. Maybe he figured someone would be tempted to listen in if she talked all night in the dining room.

Or maybe he was grateful Ruby was acting rationally, not like she had that night in his office.

She gave him her number and hung up the landline. Ignoring Connie's quizzical stare, she took the stairs two at a time, trying to decide if she'd answer when he called back or let it go to voicemail.

A full minute passed. What was he waiting for?

Finally, her phone vibrated. She let it ring three times. The last thing she wanted was to appear as desperate as she'd been that night in his office.

"Yeah?"

"Ruby? Is that you?"

Who else would it be? "I'm here." Was he going to tell her why he called or just keep her busy with stupid chitchat?

"It was, well, it was nice to see you today."

Liar. She had the decency to keep the thought to herself.

"Listen," he went on, "there's something I've been meaning to tell you. I didn't know how to get a hold of you until today. Can we talk?"

"Isn't that what we're doing?"

"Yeah," he answered. "So, this is a little awkward."

Give the doc a genius point.

"Go ahead," she said. The best they could hope for now

was to get through to the end of this conversation so they could put it out of its misery.

"I wanted to apologize. For what happened before."

Was she hearing him right? He wanted to apologize to her?

"I was totally out of line," he said.

Well, this was unexpected. He seemed ready to keep on talking, so who was she to try to stop him?

"I thought maybe if I explained things, it might help. Not to take the blame off myself. I'm not trying to make excuses. I just wanted to tell you some things about that night."

"Okay …" She sat down on her bed. This might take a while.

"You didn't know this at the time, since we only had a professional relationship, but I was engaged to someone a little bit before we met."

"Uh-huh." She had to pretend she didn't know any of this.

"It's a long, complicated story, so I'll give you the short version."

Go ahead, she wanted to say, *I heard the long version earlier.* But she just lay on her bed and stared at the vaulted ceiling.

"Amy got cancer. It was pretty aggressive. Not a whole

lot the doctors could do."

Ironic, wasn't it, that the oncologist lost his fiancée to cancer.

"She really wanted to make it to New Year's. Wanted to see the ball drop. That was kind of a big deal. We'd had our first kiss … I mean, oh never mind. I'm rambling now."

His voice had a tranquil, somewhat hypnotic sound to it. She wouldn't mind listening to it lull her to sleep.

"She passed a few weeks before that appointment with your mom …"

He didn't need to say anything else. She was sitting up now.

"I was confused. I wasn't thinking clearly. And that's why I acted so unprofessionally."

Wait a minute. He thought that night was his fault?

"The worst part is I know you were as confused and as vulnerable, and I hate to think that I was such a jerk to take advantage of you like that."

Take advantage? Apparently his memories from that night in the office were far different than hers.

She started to laugh. She couldn't help it.

"Is something funny?" he asked. "I'm being serious."

She could hear the hurt in his tone and tried to calm herself down. "I'm sorry. It's not funny. It's really not. It's just that … You really think you came on to me?"

"Isn't that how it happened?"

"Not even close. And you're right, it was totally unprofessional, and I was upset because of my mom, and I'm sure there's some sort of psychological explanation for why I acted like I did, but I knew exactly what I was doing when I asked to talk to you in your office."

He let out a little chuckle. "You did?"

"Yeah. So if you were worried about me, if you thought you'd taken advantage of some poor, helpless girl …"

"No, that's not what I meant."

"It's fine," she interrupted. She'd never admit it, but it was kind of cute that he was the one who felt guilty about that night.

"And yeah, maybe it wasn't our brightest moment," she went on, "but you were a gentleman enough to stop things when you did."

"I'm afraid I hurt your feelings," he admitted.

She laughed. "Well, you were right to put the brakes on. I would have never been able to look my mother in the eye again if we …" She stopped herself. Some things were better left unsaid.

"So you accept my apology?"

If she weren't so tired, maybe she wouldn't find this so

hysterically funny. Elliot was being earnest. She owed it to him to try to be serious. "Yes, I forgive you. And I was wrong too. I wasn't some unsuspecting victim with no choice in the matter."

"I never said you were."

"Then we can both accept our apologies and leave it at that." She had to bite her lip to keep from laughing again. He actually thought …

She shook her head in bewilderment. Wouldn't Jessi get a kick out of this? "You know what made today so awkward?" she asked. "I assumed you must think I'm some crazy, desperate woman who didn't even care that her mom was dying."

"No, that thought would have never crossed my mind. I know how hard it is to watch someone you love go through all the treatments and everything else. Neither of us were thinking clearly. I was afraid you had me pegged as a womanizing jerk for acting the way I did. I never meant to hurt you."

"Honestly?" Man, did it feel good to get the truth out for once. "Honestly," she repeated, "the only thing that hurt was how forceful you were when you put an end to things. I thought you were disgusted with me or something. I didn't think my breath smelled that bad." She let out another chuckle, less certain this time.

"No." His voice was quiet. Reflective. "No, it wasn't that. It wasn't like that at all."

CHAPTER 27

Elliot couldn't believe how nervous he'd been to make this call. It felt good to laugh about a memory that had held him in so much shame for years. He'd never told anyone about it, never mentioned how unprofessionally he'd acted, how far things almost went.

The one thing he was grateful for was this early lesson in boundaries. Maybe his early run-in with Ruby spared him from others like it in the future. His patients and their families knew he was there for them. He was supportive and compassionate, but he took pains to remain professional.

And he did his best to avoid finding himself in dark offices with young women as pretty and smart and charming as Ruby.

Her giggle in his ear was musical. When was the last time he'd laughed like this?

"So you're not mad?" he asked again, more to keep the conversation moving than because he was truly worried.

"No."

He pictured her radiant smile. The light dancing in her eyes. "I'm not mad either." He let out his breath. Relief coursed through his body like a hot beverage in the middle of a New England snowstorm.

"Great. Well, thanks for calling. I'm so glad we got that cleared up."

Wait. Was she getting ready to hang up?

He clutched his phone. What was supposed to happen now? He hadn't thought this far ahead. In fact, he hadn't hoped for this conversation to go nearly so well.

And now she was saying goodbye?

"Wait," he stammered. "Wait, what if ..." He froze. What should he say?

What if the next time you're in Seattle we find another dark office?

No, that would never do.

Elliot didn't know what to say.

"What if what?" Ruby asked. There was something mischievous in her voice. Was she teasing him?

He had to loosen his tongue. The night Amy died, she made him a promise to live. To really, truly, courageously live.

And he didn't want to let her down.

"What if we grab a bite to eat sometime?" he managed

to ask without choking on his words. "If you're ever in Seattle, I know a great place to pick up some Caesar salads."

Why did it take her so long to respond? Was she toying with him?

"I've got a better idea," she said. "Grandma Lucy's having a big birthday bash next weekend. I don't want to miss it, but I won't know anyone there. Would you like to be my date?"

He stared at his cell. Had she just one-upped him?

It was a strange feeling, but one he could most certainly get used to.

"Next weekend?" he repeated and pulled up his schedule on his phone.

"Yeah. What's wrong? You working?"

Luck was on his side. Luck or maybe providence. "No, I've got Friday and Saturday both off."

"So you'll come?" she asked.

He couldn't have wiped that stupid grin off his face to save his life. "It's a date."

CHAPTER 28

Ruby stayed on her back staring at the ceiling. She wouldn't have to go to Grandma Lucy's party all alone after all.

The only problem was she had absolutely no idea what to wear. Thank God for her best friend.

"Hello?" Jessi was breathless when she picked up. "Oh no. Is he already there? Has he already left?"

Ruby stared at the phone. It was Jessi's voice, but she had no idea what she was talking about.

"What?"

Jessi cleared her throat and responded with an innocent, "Oh, never mind. Thought you were someone else. What's up?"

Ruby checked to make sure her door was shut. The stupid attic room didn't even have a lock, but thankfully the stairs were enough of a deterrent that the old people here hardly ever came up.

"You know how Grandma Lucy has that big birthday

party? And I'm supposed to go, but I feel stupid since I don't know anyone in her huge family?"

"Yeah?"

Ruby couldn't contain her giggle. "Well, you'll never believe what I did. I got myself a date."

"What?" Jessi snapped. "So he is there."

"I have no idea what you're talking about. But did you hear me?" Ruby was almost squealing. "I've got a date."

"Oh, that's great." Wait a minute. Why was Jessi acting all reserved now?

"Listen, if you're still upset about me and Mace, you've got to remember, we talked about it when we first started dating again …"

"Oh, I remember," Jessi interrupted. "Sisters before misters. Of course. It's not that. It really isn't. It's just …"

There was a knock on the front door. Who would be coming by the farmhouse this late?

"It's just that …" Since when had Jessi ever forgotten how to talk?

"Ruby!" Connie called from downstairs. "Oh, Ruby! A young man's here to see you."

Uh-oh.

"It's just that," Jessi tried one more time, but Ruby cut her off.

"Listen, someone's here. I've got to go."

"Yeah, about that," Jessi began before Ruby threw her phone on the bed and rushed out of her room.

CHAPTER 29

She nearly tripped on the stairs when she saw him standing in the entryway.

"Mace?"

"Ruby."

Connie was already in her nightgown and curlers. "I'll let you two talk, but I want you to stay down here with the lights on at all times. You two got that?"

Ruby ignored her. She was too busy staring at Mace. "What are you doing here?" she asked once she found her voice.

"I wanted to talk to you."

Ruby had to sit down. "Come in."

She pulled a chair out from the dining room table. He did the same.

"They go to bed really early here," she lectured. "You should have called or something."

He smiled at her. Man, she loved that sheepish grin he'd get when he thought she was mad. "I guess I wanted to give you a surprise."

"Well, I'm surprised. What do you want?" Her heart pounded. What was he doing here? Did he already know about Elliot? But how could he have found out so fast unless …

Jessi.

She sighed.

He fidgeted with his hands. How many energy drinks had he chugged down on the drive out here? "I wanted to talk to you."

She shrugged, trying to act like she didn't care. "I've got ears. Talk."

He cleared his throat. "I wanted to tell you that I miss you. And that I'm sorry."

Sorry? There was something new. "Sorry for what?"

"For pushing you away. For not trying harder to make things work out between us when you …" He stopped himself, and she knew exactly why.

He wasn't going to wiggle off this hook so easily.

"When I what?"

"When you got all churchy on me."

Was he accusing her?

She bit her lip. Tried to shrug again, but she wasn't sure it was as convincing this time. "People change. You should know that."

"I know. And I've thought about it, and I'm really happy for you. Happy you've found something that makes you feel good after your mom died."

She clenched her jaw shut to keep from interrupting him. Her mother had nothing to do with this, but the longer he talked, the bigger a hole he could dig himself into. The less guilty she'd feel for having a date lined up next weekend with Elliot the medical school graduate. Elliot the oncologist.

Elliot who was every bit the handsome, respectable, totally desirable man Ruby told Jessi about so many years ago.

Mace was staring at the table. He was so unattractive when he didn't know what to say. "I guess what I wanted to tell you is I'm cool with you being a Christian, that's all."

"You're cool with it?" Her tone was icy now. She had regained her composure and seized the upper hand. "I don't remember asking your permission, did I?"

"No, but maybe that was the problem."

"Excuse me?" Was she really hearing him right?

"No, I mean, maybe that sounded bad, but really, we've never made any major decision without talking it over."

"I didn't realize I needed you to sign off on my religious

beliefs."

He shook his head. She was glad she was making him uncomfortable. The jerk deserved it.

"That's not what I'm saying. Listen. I came here to tell you I'm happy for you. Did you hear me? And I'm sorry. For not being more supportive when you first started changing."

"Why does everyone say I changed?" Ruby blurted out. "You, Jessi, you're all talking about how I'm this totally new person since I met Grandma Lucy, but it's not like that. You're the one who changed." Good. Now the awkwardness had turned to rage. That she could handle. What she couldn't handle were the people closest to her complaining about how she'd turned into some brand-new person the minute she prayed with Grandma Lucy to ask Jesus to forgive her sins.

"What are you talking about?" Mace glowered at her. Man, he had a temper. What had she seen in him all those years? "I didn't change. I'm the one finishing up college so we could get engaged and get you and my little sis out of Orchard Grove."

"What's wrong with Orchard Grove?" she shouted. No, this wouldn't work. She had to remember everyone else was trying to get to sleep. "There's nothing wrong with Orchard Grove," she insisted more quietly this time. "I've been perfectly happy here. You were the one all intent on up and moving."

"Because there's no life for us here."

"There's no life for us anywhere," she snapped back. What part of broken up didn't he get? She shook her head. "Listen, I guess some girls might think it's sweet that you drove all the way out here just to try to convince me to take you back, but seriously, it creeps me out. We're through."

"Does this have something to do with that guy from Seattle?"

"What?" So Jessi had told him about Elliot. Her and her big mouth. Ruby hoped that by the time she was done yelling at Mace, she'd have enough energy left to call Jessi and let her know what she thought. Some best friend. No wonder she'd acted all strange on the phone.

"Jessi put you up to this." It made so much sense now.

"No she didn't." He'd always been a pathetic liar. "Just listen to me." At least now he was talking calmly. "Let's just start everything over. Back it up."

"It's a little late for that."

"Just humor me."

She crossed her arms. "Fine."

This better be good.

Mace took a deep breath. The two of them had been together for so long she could read each and every stress sign on his body. His jittery leg. His darting eyes. The way his jaw twitched when he started talking.

"Okay. Let me say what I have to say and then I'll be gone."

"Good."

"No interrupting. Please."

She glared at him.

"Thank you. Now listen. A few months ago, you had this great religious experience that convinced you God is real and Jesus is your homeboy, and I didn't say a word against it. Yeah, I was a little nervous. I wasn't exactly sure where things would go, but I was willing to work it out. You gave me some rules about how far we could go before we got married, and I didn't complain too much. I may be a dude, but I know how to respect boundaries. And I did.

"Then you started meeting more and more with this Grandma Lucy of yours, and you and me couldn't hang out late anymore on Saturdays because you had to be up early for church, and that was fine. You didn't hear a word from me about it. Not one little word."

She had a couple examples to prove him otherwise, but she didn't want to drag out this conversation any longer than was absolutely necessary.

"All right," she said, and he held up his hand as if those

two words might be enough to throw off his concentration.

"All these things were changing, and I was just being my happy-go-lucky self, going with the flow because hey, I'm the kind of guy who knows how to support his girlfriend, right? But then you come to me and instead of saying you're breaking up with me right away, you say you're thinking about breaking up with me because this Grandma Lucy of yours says it wouldn't be right for a Christian to date a non-Christian.

"You didn't ask me what I thought about church. You didn't ask me what I believed about God. You just told me that since I wasn't doing all the exact same things you were that I wasn't good enough for you."

"Wait a minute. I never said …"

"Let me finish," Mace interrupted. "I'm almost done. I was mad. I won't deny that. But you know what? More than that I was hurt." He stared at her as if he were convinced she could read the pain in his expression.

She could.

"I wasn't hurt because you were thinking about leaving me. I was hurt because you didn't even ask me if I would change for you. As if you just expected me to be some stupid, stubborn Neanderthal who wouldn't even be able to understand what you believed in because you never explained it to me. I mean, come on. You were all excited about your new Jesus thing, about going to church and all that junk, and never once did you ask me if I wanted to go with you."

Ruby blinked at him. "Would you have come?"

"I don't know, but you didn't even give me the choice. Do you know how much that hurt me?"

She lowered her eyes. She had talked with Jessi a little bit about her new faith, explained salvation to her, but Jessi was so apathetic Ruby was sure her brother would be even less interested. "I had no idea."

"Because you weren't thinking. I swear that woman's bewitched you or something. You dove headfirst into the whole Jesus thing, and you stopped thinking about me. It'd be like if all I could talk about was some big party they were having on campus, and I didn't even think to invite you there. I just kept railing on and on about how much I was looking forward to it, and never once did I say, *Hey, Ruby, you think you want to come too*?"

He shook his head. He didn't have to tell her how upset he was.

She could hear it in his voice.

"I'm really sorry."

"You know what's the worst? I've been studying some

of Christianity. Even went over to the campus chapel, and I made myself an appointment to talk to the chaplain there."

She was shaking now. Why was she shaking?

"You did?"

"Yeah. I figured if you weren't going to explain it to me, then I needed someone who could. I needed someone to explain to me what could be so stinking important that you'd treat me like garbage just to grab hold of it."

"I didn't treat you like that," she stammered, but he kept on going like he didn't hear.

"You know what that chaplain told me? He said that people who don't believe in Jesus go to hell. Don't stop me. I need to get this out because this is what really got me. He said that as a Christian, you would believe that I'd go to hell if I didn't repent or do whatever it is you do when you turn yourself into a believer. Is that true?"

He stared at her.

She couldn't answer.

"Is that true?"

What did he want her to say?

"Because if it is," he went on, "if you honestly believe that I'm going to hell unless I convert like you — and I'm not saying I believe all that junk, I'm still trying to sort it out on my own — but if you believe that's the truth, then why in the world wouldn't you try to tell me?"

"I didn't want to make you uncomfortable." Even when she said the words she knew what a pitiful excuse she was making.

"Uncomfortable? No." He was standing up now, stomping up and down the dining room. "Uncomfortable is how you feel when it's ninety degrees out and you don't got air conditioning. Uncomfortable is how you feel when you go to the dentist and they've got to numb you up before they drill. But this, this hell that you all of a sudden believe in, that's a whole lot different than uncomfortable. I can't believe you wouldn't even think to ask me if I wanted to save myself from a fate like that. I thought we were friends."

These last words wounded her even more than their breakup had.

He was right.

They were friends.

Best friends.

Not in the same way she and Jessi were. With Mace it was different. It was love and friendship and romance and passion and an entire lifetime of shared memories. And she hadn't even thought to ask him if he wanted to learn more about her newfound faith?

He shook his head and shoved his hand into his pocket.

"I came here to apologize. To tell you I'm sorry for not being as supportive as I should have been when you were all excited about your conversion. But now I don't even know what I am. To think that you'd care that little for me …"

"That's not what it is." Her throat threatened to clench shut. She had to make him understand.

"Then what is it?"

"I didn't want you to become a Christian just for me." She swallowed. She had to get through this. "I didn't want you to say you believed in God just so we could keep on being together. It doesn't work like that."

"What do you mean it doesn't work like that? Isn't that how it happened with you and that Grandma Lucy chick?"

Ruby blinked, defying her tears. She wouldn't cry. Not now. "When Grandma Lucy and I were talking, something happened in my heart. I could feel it."

"So you're telling me that until God gives me some touchy-feely willies, I can't be saved?"

"No."

"That if I don't feel something about him I can't become a genuine believer?"

"That's not what I'm saying."

"Then what are you saying? Because I'd really like to know. I'd like to know why you're keeping this little church-girl thing all to yourself, why you cut me out of your life without even asking me how I felt about it, how this God of yours is so important you'd throw everything we had between us out the window. Because if he's that good, if this Christian thing is that much of a joyride, I want it. Did you hear me? I want it. Because let me tell you something. Growing up in a stupid, podunk town full of narrow-minded, hypocritical people was bad enough. Don't you think I've got problems? Don't you think I'd sometimes like to have some heavenly Father up in the clouds to tell about all my worries and all my fears? Don't you think I've got questions? Like why your mom died of cancer, or why as hard as I've worked to get ahead in life I'm nothing more than a sixth-year senior? Don't you think I'd like someone to talk to about those things?"

"You could talk to me," she told him lamely. "You could always talk to me."

"Yeah, but then you changed. You got all churchy and you didn't want me to follow where you went."

"It wasn't that. I didn't want to ask you to change for me."

"Then why else do people change? Why did you start wearing makeup when you were in seventh grade? Huh? Isn't it because my sister told you it was the thing everyone was doing? Why did you take that semester off nursing school to care for your mom at the end? Why do we do anything in this stupid, pointless universe? It's because we care about people. We make those changes because we care about people. Just like I cared about you."

She couldn't make him understand. This wasn't about her anymore. It was about him. About his desire to know if God was real or not. And she'd been so reserved she hadn't even asked him if he wanted to talk about her faith.

"I'm sorry." She was almost whispering.

"Come again?"

What did he want her to do? Get down on her knees? "I said I'm sorry. For not talking to you more about God. For assuming you wouldn't want to listen. For ..." She swallowed down the lump in her throat. "For pushing you away instead of asking you if you wanted to have a relationship with Jesus." She forced herself to meet his gaze. "Do you?"

They stared at each other. It felt like an eternity.

"Do you?" she repeated.

He shook his head. "I don't know."

She let out her breath. All this lecture and he still didn't know. Great. Then why was he yelling at her if he hadn't even made up his mind yet? She couldn't do this anymore.

Not tonight. She was too tired.

"Listen, I've got to head to bed. Everyone gets up early around here."

"Can I call you?" he asked.

"What?"

"Can I call you? When I'm back on campus?"

"Sure. Whatever." She paused before she headed upstairs. "I mean, sure. Go ahead and call. It sounds like we have a lot to talk about."

"Yeah." He looked as exhausted as she was. "I guess we do."

CHAPTER 30

Elliot knew he would regret staying up so late, but he had to talk to someone. He paced his apartment with his hands-free set on.

"And then she said, *I've got a better idea. Why don't you come here next weekend because Grandma Lucy's got a big birthday party and I need to find a date.*"

His foster sister giggled. "That is so sweet."

"I know. I mean, all I did was ask her out to dinner the next time she was in Seattle, and you know how that could have gone. Months could have passed, and nothing. But she didn't just set the time, she called it a real live date."

"I'm happy for you," Tiff said.

"I know. I can't even think about going to sleep."

"I can tell."

He and his foster sister had reconnected after running into each other in Seattle when her little girl was in the NICU. She and her husband and their daughter lived in Seattle now, and they all got together a few times a month.

He suspected some of it had to do with Tiff's still feeling ill-prepared to parent a baby as medically fragile as Natalie, and even though he was no pediatrician, Elliot was happy to offer what advice he could. They'd all gone together to watch Fourth of July fireworks last summer, even baby Natalie with her feeding tube and oxygen tank, and Elliot actually felt like he was part of a family.

For once.

"What are you going to wear?" Tiff asked.

"Wear?"

"Yeah. You know. They do wear clothes to old ladies' birthday parties, right?"

He smiled. "Right. What do you suggest?"

"Don't ask me. I'd show up in my sweat pants and hoodie."

He laughed. "I'll think of something."

"I'm sure you will. And hey, you know what?"

"No. What?"

"I'm really excited for you."

He shook his head. "You're just being cheesy now."

"No, I mean it. After all you've gone through, you really deserve someone to make you happy. I'm glad the two of you ran into each other today."

"Yeah. Me too."

"And I'm glad you got the chance to explain to her that you're not some freaky, perverted predator."

He laughed again, although a little less certain this time. "Right." He knew Tiff's sense of humor. Knew before long he'd regret telling her this whole story.

But it still felt good to talk with someone.

"How's Jake, by the way?" he asked.

"Oh, he's fine. He's hanging out with Natalie now."

"She's still awake?"

Tiff sighed. "Yeah, the doctors put her on this new med. It knocks her out during the day, so we're up with her until pretty late at night. But hey, good news is no more seizures."

He was glad to hear the optimism in her tone. It had taken several months before Tiff could talk about her daughter with any sort of emotion in her voice.

It had been great catching up with her, but it was late. "Well," he said, "I've got to go. Tell Jake hi for me and give that cutie of yours a big, sloppy kiss."

"I will. Oh, one more thing. You have Thanksgiving plans?"

"No. Not yet. Why?"

"Come on over. I'll be making my very first turkey. I've been practicing with whole chickens, you know. I'm getting pretty good at it."

"Sure." He couldn't keep from smiling. "Thanksgiving sounds great. Thanks, Tiff."

He could hear the smile in her voice. "Goodnight, Elly."

She was the only person who could use his childhood nickname without making it sound insulting. He grinned and hung up the phone, thinking about that promise he'd made to his fiancée the night she died.

It took him a few years, but maybe he was finally learning to live the way Amy wanted him to.

CHAPTER 31

"What do you mean, you didn't talk to Mace?" Ruby had just finished lunch and was taking a quick break upstairs while Grandma Lucy napped in her prayer chair.

"I mean exactly what I said." The kids in Jessi's daycare were supposed to be napping too, so she was keeping her voice down. "I didn't tell him anything."

"Then how did he know about Elliot?"

"Who?"

"The doctor," Ruby hissed. "The one from Seattle."

Jessi was quiet. "Oh."

"Oh?" Her best friend had potentially ruined her life and all she could say was *Oh?*

"Yeah, I think I maybe mentioned it to him. But only because it was so weird that you hadn't seen him in all these years and then he popped up where you work. I mean, don't you think that's a strange coincidence?"

"Whatever I think it is, you promised me you weren't going to interfere or try to set me and Mace up again. I thought you understood."

Jessi sighed. "He's my brother. What did you expect me to do?"

"Keep your word and mind your own business." Ruby was sulking, but she wasn't about to make excuses for her behavior.

Jessi was totally out of line. "Well, if it makes you feel any better, he's gone now."

"What do you mean he's gone?" Ruby asked.

"I mean gone. Back to campus. He left last night."

"Why wouldn't he?" Mace was still in college, wasn't he? He was still planning on getting his degree at some point in the future, right?

Jessi huffed. "Listen, I've got to go. I've got one kid yelling for me to help her wash her hands in the bathroom, I've got another who keeps kicking his sister's cot, and there's a new toddler who literally hasn't stopped screaming for his mom all day."

Now that she mentioned it, Jessi did sound pretty tired.

Ruby let out her breath. "Go do what you've got to do." She thought back over their conversation. Had they seriously gone ten minutes without Jessi complaining about her work or snapping at the kids?

"All right," Jessi said. "Come over tonight. Let's hang

out."

Ruby didn't have the heart to argue. "Fine."

"I'll see you then. And hey," Jessi added, "I'm sorry. For blabbing about Dr. Hottie and not telling you Mace was coming to town. It was bad timing, and you know me. I still really want to see the two of you together. You and Mace, I mean. Not the doctor. But if you want me to get Mr. Seattle Casual off your hands at that old lady's party …"

Ruby smiled. "I'm not switching anything. I really want to get to know Elliot better, and I want you to be okay with that. No, not just okay with it. I want you to be happy for me."

Jessi hesitated on the other end. "Yeah, okay."

"What's that mean?"

"Yeah, I'm happy for you. Whoever you end up with. Even though you know it's gotta be my brother."

Ruby chuckled, but her heart wasn't in it. Why did Jessi sound so tired? Maybe Mace had kept her up all night.

She and Jessi definitely needed some girl time together.

This evening couldn't come soon enough.

CHAPTER 32

Elliot couldn't remember a longer shift. Was that how the entire week would go before he returned to Orchard Grove?

It wasn't like him. He'd gone on exactly two dates since Amy died. One was with her sister who was as different from Amy as Seattle was from Orchard Grove. They'd ended the night with no hard feelings but with the very clear understanding that they'd never go out and preferably never talk to each other again.

The second date was someone his foster sister Tiff set him up with, some girlfriend of hers who lived nearby. It wasn't technically a disaster, but he dropped her off at home right after dinner, and neither of them mentioned getting together again.

The night Amy died, he'd thought it was cruel for her to mention his finding happiness in a world she was leaving. How could he ever experience joy again? But now he realized her words were a blessing. It was all right to move on.

He didn't have to feel guilty.

He thought about Amy, wondering if she and Ruby would have liked each other. His fiancée was quiet, sensitive. Elliot got the feeling Ruby was far more loud and outgoing, maybe even brash.

Had his tastes changed?

They didn't look alike either. Amy had been blond. Thin, even before the cancer hit.

Ruby had dark hair, nearly black. Feminine curves, a strong presence.

Would the two have liked each other? Maybe. But they certainly wouldn't have been soulmates.

Had he made a mistake? No. This was the right thing. The right time. Ruby was the first person to ever ask him out. Apparently, scrawny boys with asthma aren't first pickings for homecoming or prom, and by the time Elliot hit college he was too busy studying to care much about dating.

Dating. The word sounded weird. He almost felt too old for it. Not that he expected to remain single his entire life. Then again, when he made the drive all the way out to Orchard Grove to meet Grandma Lucy, he hadn't planned to return the next week for a woman.

A very pretty woman with a large smile and lips that he

remembered being so soft …

No, he didn't want to think about that. Their first romantic encounter was a mistake. This was a time for a new beginning.

A fresh start.

If he didn't die of impatience before the weekend came.

CHAPTER 33

"Grandma Lucy?" Ruby leaned over to shake the old woman awake. "Grandma Lucy?"

She had never napped this long. Ruby should have checked on her nearly an hour ago. What had she been doing upstairs? Had she and Jessi been yakking that whole time?

"Grandma Lucy?"

Her eyes fluttered open, and even before she opened her mouth, Ruby could tell it would be one of the bad afternoons. The kind of work day that cured her of feeling guilty for taking up so much of Connie's out-of-pocket money while they waited for the insurance paperwork to come through.

She held the old woman's hand. "How do you feel?"

"Mom?"

She shook her head. "No. I'm Ruby. I'm your nurse."

Grandma Lucy broke out into a soft smile. "Isn't that nice? You're awfully young to be a nurse, aren't you?"

"Are you tired?" Ruby asked. "You were sleeping a long time."

"I was? What's Mom doing?"

"She's not here right now. She wanted me to take care of you for a little bit." Ruby wondered what Grandma Lucy would say about this little white lie if she were in her right mind.

"That's nice. What did you say your name was?"

"I'm Ruby."

"Well, I'm happy to meet you, Ruby. Do you know Jesus as your personal Lord and Savior? Have I told you about the day I was saved?"

"Yes, you've told me."

"So you're born-again?

Ruby understood why Connie hired her. It was hard enough for Ruby to see Grandma Lucy acting so confused. It must be more difficult for someone like Connie, who'd lived with her for decades.

"Yes, I'm born again, thanks to you."

"What do you mean thanks to me?"

"I mean you're the one who first told me about Jesus. Don't you remember?" She bit her lip. She had to stop using that phrase.

Grandma Lucy shook her head. "I'm afraid I don't. But did you know that when a sinner comes to repentance, the angels in heaven rejoice?"

"I did know that. You're the one who told me."

"I did?"

"Mm-hmm."

"Well, I suppose I'm having a hard time remembering."

"That's okay. Are you ready for a snack?"

"What did you say?"

Ruby leaned down toward Grandma Lucy's ear. "A snack. Do you want something to eat?"

"Did Mom make her bread rolls?"

"I'm not sure." She sighed. It was the nurse's curse — being born with a heavy dose of compassion that you had to temper if you hoped to remain even slightly productive. If Ruby stopped to mourn over every single thing Grandma Lucy forgot on days like this, she'd never get anything done.

"Can I help you get into your wheelchair?" she asked.

"I have a wheelchair?"

"Yup. It's a nice sturdy one." With practiced movements, she eased Grandma Lucy into it. "Careful now."

Grandma Lucy sat stroking the arm rest like it were a pet. "This is nice."

Ruby forced cheer into her voice. "It's yours."

"I like it."

"I'm glad." Ruby wheeled her out of her prayer room and toward the dining room.

"We're going to the doctor?" Grandma Lucy asked.

"No, no doctors today. It's time for a snack."

"I thought you said there was a doctor here."

Ruby wheeled the chair up to the table and put on the brakes. "That was yesterday. Dr. Jameson. He sat right where you are."

"Here in this chair?"

"No, not in the chair, but by where you're sitting now."

"That was nice. Did he give me a check-out?"

"You mean a checkup?"

Grandma Lucy nodded and glanced around the room as if she hadn't seen it before.

"No, he wasn't here to give you a checkup," Ruby answered.

"Oh, I thought he was. I'm not feeling too well."

It was the first time, on a good day or a bad one, that Grandma Lucy admitted to any sort of discomfort or concern.

Ruby stared at her carefully. "What's not feeling right?" She took Grandma Lucy's hand casually in hers but worked her way carefully up to her wrist to check her pulse.

"I thought I was sick, and that could explain the nightmares."

"You're having nightmares?" It was the first Ruby had

heard about them. "What about?"

"Fire."

"Fire?"

Grandma Lucy nodded. "People crying. Lots of mamas worried about their babies."

"Well, you don't have to worry about any fire now. Everything's just …"

The landline phone rang. Ruby let it go to the old-fashioned answering machine.

Connie's voice filled the room, at least the mechanical version of it. "Thank you for calling Safe Anchorage Goat Farms, where you come in as a friend and walk out as family."

"Who's that?" Grandma Lucy looked around. Her eyes were wide, and she clutched Ruby's hand.

"That's Connie. Your niece."

"I have a niece?"

Ruby nodded. Grandma Lucy hadn't had a day this bad in weeks.

The answering machine beeped.

"Ruby? Ruby? Are you there? Pick up right now."

She froze. Mace? How had he gotten this number? Why was he calling here? Why did he sound so panicked?

"Ruby, pick up the phone for the love of everything holy. Something happened. Jessi's hurt."

CHAPTER 34

Mace

I don't understand it. It can't be happening. None of this is real.

It's a dream. That's all it is. One terrible, horrible, no good, very bad dream. Isn't there a movie about something like that?

I should have never driven all the way back to campus. They tell me that Jessi's on her way to Seattle, the totally opposite side of the state from me. It'll take me four or five hours to get there.

I can hardly drive. I'm so jittery. I'm not even sure I've got the gas money to make it, but that's the least of my worries right now.

She's got to be okay. She's got to.

I don't know if there's a God, and if there is, I honestly can't come up with one good reason why he'd care to do this for me, but he's got to hear me. I've never prayed before, not like this. I think sometimes we remember to say grace at Thanksgiving, you know where you all hold hands and talk about what you're grateful for. And sure, when I'm about to take a test or something, I might pray how I hope I'll pass, but this is different.

I'm begging God. Which is funny, because an hour ago if you'd asked me, I wouldn't have been able to tell you if I even believed in him or not, but I do now.

I've got to.

Who else is going to make any of this all right?

Who else is going to get me all the way to Seattle on time?

Who else is going to keep my sister alive?

CHAPTER 35

There were three ambulance vehicles in front of County Hospital when Ruby pulled up. Until then, she didn't even know there were that many ambulances in all of Orchard Grove.

She parked in front of the main entrance since the emergency area was blocked.

God, she prayed, *please let her be okay.*

She told Connie what happened as soon as she got off that phone call. Her employer gave her the rest of the day off even though Grandma Lucy was doing so poorly. It was just as well, or Ruby would have simply quit her job to be here.

It didn't make sense.

None of this made sense.

And more than anything, Jessi couldn't die.

It wasn't possible.

Ruby hurried into the building, ignoring the faces around her, the moving bodies, the bustling nurses who a few months ago had been her co-workers.

"Where's Jessi?" she asked a tall man in scrubs. She recognized him but couldn't find the space in her brain to try to recall his name.

He frowned. "Are you one of the parents?"

She didn't have a clue what he was talking about. "Where's Jessi? Have they brought her in yet?"

He pointed down the hall. "Check in with the front desk in the emergency lobby."

Her lungs were bursting by the time she arrived. She could barely tell the triage nurse her friend's name.

"Is she here?" *Dear God,* she prayed, *please let her still be alive.*

The nurse shook her head. "She's on her way to Seattle. To the burn center there."

Ruby listened to the words as if they were coming at her through six feet of water. The burn center? Seattle?

"But she's going to be okay?" Ruby blurted. "She'll be all right?"

The nurse frowned at her. What happened to telling the truth? What happened to professional courtesy?

This was ridiculous. "You aren't family, are you?" the nurse asked.

Ruby had to clear her brain. "She's my sister-in-law. Well, almost. I'm engaged to her brother. And she's been my best friend since kindergarten." Were those tears about to streak down her face? No, she didn't need those. Even if she were trying to make her lie more convincing.

"I'm sorry," the nurse whispered. "I don't know a whole lot more than you, but the burns were pretty bad."

So what? Pretty bad could mean touching your finger against the oven rack and getting a blister.

People didn't die from *pretty bad.*

Especially not Jessi.

A woman stumbled into the lobby. "Where's Bowman?" she sobbed. "Help me, dear God, and someone please tell me where my baby is."

Ruby glanced around. Had she ever seen it so crowded in here? The worried faces, the somber expressions of her former co-workers.

Just how bad was it?

She hadn't realized she asked the question out loud.

"Real bad," the triage nurse responded.

"Where's Bowman? Where's my baby?" The mother collapsed into a chair, and someone rushed to her side.

A fire truck pulled up in front of the entryway, wailing its sirens.

There was nothing for Ruby to do here.

"You say they took her to Seattle?"

The nurse nodded. "Yeah. The plane left twenty minutes ago or so."

"Okay." Ruby did the math in her head. She could start driving now. By the time she arrived, Jessi would be settled in.

Stabilized.

And on the road to a perfect recovery.

It had to be that way.

It just had to.

CHAPTER 36

Elliot glanced up from his cottage cheese and cantaloupe lunch and pulled his cell out of his pocket. Who was texting him in the middle of the day?

Could it be Ruby? He'd been trying to decide all day if he should text her now or later. He wanted to stay in touch, but he was afraid of appearing too desperate.

This message was from his foster sister.

Did you hear about the fire in Orchard Grove?

Fire? What fire? He jumped straight to his internet browser. He didn't want to wait for Tiff to text him all the details.

Gas explosion in Orchard Grove daycare wounds six kids and one worker.

Oh no.

He browsed the first few paragraphs about the daycare fire then skipped ahead.

Local daycare worker, Jessi Lacasa, age 24, is being heralded a hero after calmly leading the children in her care to safety.

"Jessi is one of the most dedicated workers our center has seen," said Denise Sharpton, owner of Orchard Grove Play'n'Learn. "She's always putting the children first. Today was just one example of many."

After noticing that one of the daycare center children was unaccounted for, Lacasa returned to the burning building to look for him.

"One of the little boys was stuck in the bathroom," Sharpton said. "But Jessi ran right in after him, carried him out in her arms. They were both badly burned."

As of this writing, all of the children are being treated locally and are in stable condition. After rescuing the child trapped in the bathroom, Lacasa was flown to the Seattle Burn Center for treatment.

This is an ongoing story ...

Elliot shook his head. What a tragedy. He'd definitely have to check in with Ruby soon, see if she knew any of the families involved, see if there was anything he could do to help.

His pager beeped. Lunch was over.

He had to get back to his shift.

CHAPTER 37

Ruby had never driven so recklessly. Good thing it was still fall. No snow or ice on the mountain pass, although not even deplorable road conditions would keep her away from her best friend's side.

She'd been calling Mace every five or ten minutes, but he wasn't getting any more updates than she was. That was a good sign, right? If something really bad happened, the doctors would tell Jessi's brother.

Wouldn't they?

Mace had to drive all the way from Spokane, so Ruby had a head start on him.

What had Jessi been thinking? Why had she gone back into that building?

No, that was a stupid question to ask. Jessi had acted more heroically than Ruby would have ever given her credit for. If it hadn't been for Jessi's courage, that little boy might have died.

Ruby's throat stung. Why did God let Jessi get hurt? He

should be rewarding her for her selflessness, not making her suffer.

And burns …

Ruby had only spent one week's rotation in the burn ward during nursing school. There was a reason it had the highest turnover rate of any other unit. If there were only a way she could get the screams of those patients out of her mind …

Okay God, you've got to help Jessi. You've got to.

It was all the praying she could do. She was no Grandma Lucy. She couldn't sit for hours just talking to the Lord the same way she and Jessi could spend hours gabbing away. Ruby was new to the whole faith thing, new to prayer, new to hope.

And if God let her best friend die …

She wouldn't think that way.

God, please help her.

She'd never prayed more sincerely about anything in her life, and even though her prayer wasn't flowery or expressive like Grandma Lucy's always were, Ruby hoped heaven would hear anyway.

Hear and act.

Because there was no way she was going to lose her best friend.

And if she did, she'd never forgive the God who took her away.

CHAPTER 38

Another long shift over. Elliot tried to decide if he wanted to pick up his dinner at the hospital cafeteria or eat what he had at home. There was still some hummus left. He'd have to finish that up in the next couple days. And he was low on fruit. Probably needed to pick up some more groceries at the health food store. Soon, but not tonight.

He walked downstairs to the cafeteria. "Hi, Mo," he told the janitor wiping the tables.

Mo grinned, showing the gap between his two front teeth. "Hi, Doctor. Did you have a good day?"

The thing Elliot had learned about talking to Mo was to have his ears prepared. That man was either silent or screaming.

"My day was good," Elliot answered. "How was yours?"

"Miss Lopez says I'm still the best worker she's ever had." He smiled proudly.

Elliot would have given him a friendly pat on the back or offered to shake his hand, but he knew Mo didn't like to be touched. "That's great. Miss Lopez is right. Before you started working here, they never could get these tables to shine."

"You getting some dinner, Doctor?" Mo asked.

Elliot nodded. "Yeah. You want something?"

Mo looked at his watch, disappointed. "No. I have thirty-seven more minutes before I take my next break. Miss Lopez gets mad if I finish early."

"Well, I don't want you to get in trouble with Miss Lopez," Elliot said, even though he knew Mo's supervisor was about as intimidating as a baby hedgehog. "See you later, Mo."

He made his way to the salad bar and started filling his plate.

Just a few weeks before he returned to Orchard Grove.

To Ruby.

Thinking about her reminded him of the terrible fire at that daycare. He'd kept himself updated between his rounds, and apparently there'd been some issue about a potential gas leak the owner of the daycare allegedly knew about for weeks but still hadn't taken care of. She'd be lucky if she got through this ordeal with a single penny left to her name.

With as much as he had to pay for malpractice insurance, Elliot hated the way this country was so litigation-happy, but when it came to putting innocent children at risk, it was a good thing he'd never sit on that jury if the daycare owner were charged with criminal negligence. There was nothing that made him angrier than watching children suffer.

He needed to talk to Ruby. See how she was. In a town that small, a tragedy could impact everyone.

He sat down at one of the recently wiped tables. Mo was in the far corner of the room, but Elliot could hear him whistling all the way from where he sat.

Elliot pulled out his phone.

Time to check in with Ruby.

CHAPTER 39

She jumped when the phone rang. She'd been paying attention to the road, hadn't she?

So why was she so startled?

She glanced at the time. Mace should have called her half an hour ago with an update.

"Hello?"

"Hi, Ruby. It's me. Elliot."

"Who?" Where was Mace? Why hadn't he checked in?

"Elliot. You know." He lowered his voice. "Dr. Jameson."

"Yeah, hi. I'm sorry, now's a really bad time." Where was she? How long had she been driving with her brain turned off? She had to stay alert. Had to get to Seattle.

"Everything okay?"

What kind of question was that? "No. It's not."

"I'm so sorry. Anything I can do to …"

Another beep. There was Mace. The idiot. Why had he kept her waiting so long?

"Sorry, Elliot." She almost dropped the phone trying to hang up. "I've got another call coming in. Got to take this one. Bye."

Why couldn't she ever remember which button she was supposed to push? "Hello? Mace? That you?"

"It's still me."

The doctor. Rats. "Okay, I'm going to try again." Another swipe of the screen. There. This time it worked.

"Mace? Where are you? Why didn't you call earlier? Mace? You there?"

"I'm here."

"You sound awful. Are you on something?"

"No." His voice was flat. "No, I haven't had anything."

"Where are you at?" she demanded.

"I'm not sure. I've been on this same road forever …"

"You sound like you're about to fall asleep."

"No, I'm not." Great. She knew that droopy sound in his voice.

"Mace." She was practically screaming to get his attention. "Mace!"

"What? I'm right here."

"No, you're not. You're totally out of it. Now find a shoulder to pull over into and take a nap."

"I've got to get to Jessi…" He was slurring nearly as

badly as he had when she picked him up from the dentist after getting his wisdom teeth out, except this time there was nothing funny about his lethargic responses.

"You'll be no help to your sister dead. So pull over, take a nap, then find yourself some coffee or one of those disgusting energy drinks the next place you can."

"I thought you said they'd rot my teeth and give me cancer."

"They probably will," she replied, "but at least you'll make it to Seattle alive."

Sheesh. She should have waited for him to get to Orchard Grove where he could have picked her up on the way. What good was saving a few hours if he ended up dead?

"Come on. Have you found a shoulder yet?"

"Yeah."

"Then why do I still hear your car running?"

"I haven't turned it off yet."

"Just take a nap, and call me when you wake up, all right? And get one of those stupid energy drinks. Get ten if you have to. Just don't drive anymore until you've had some rest."

"I'm not that tired."

"Just shut up, pull over, and sleep." She ended the call. Fabulous. Now in addition to worrying about Jessi in Seattle, probably screaming and writhing in pain, she had to think about Mace, who was the most irresponsible, juvenile driver she'd ever met. He was making this trip dog-tired and was just as likely to fall asleep behind the wheel and get himself killed as he was to make it to Seattle.

She couldn't handle it. *Do you hear that, God? I can't deal with all this stress.*

It was too much for her. She needed something. Some kind of a diversion. Someone she could talk to.

She stared at her phone. Should she? She'd feel like an idiot. But maybe it would make the drive pass more quickly. And since he was a doctor and worked at the Seattle hospital, he might have some way to tell her how Jessi was doing.

Besides, she owed him an explanation for the way she'd hung up on him a few minutes ago.

She sighed. How many bites of humble pie would she have to eat?

She shook her head. Well, it was better than nothing. Besides, she hated to admit it, but she was nearly as tired as Mace and probably just as dangerous on the road.

She could use a distraction. Something to focus on besides her anxiety.

She picked up her phone and made the call.

"Hi, Elliot. It's Ruby."

CHAPTER 40

Elliot was on his way to the parking garage when Ruby returned his call. "Everything all right?" he asked. She sounded worried.

Worried and incredibly tired.

"It's been a crazy day."

"Yeah, I heard about that fire at the daycare."

"It was my best friend."

He stopped hunting for his keys. "What?"

"My best friend. The worker at the daycare who got burned so bad."

Oh, no. "Ruby, I'm sorry. I had no idea. Is she all right? What have you heard?" He felt guilty for going the entire day without knowing.

"Nothing," Ruby answered. "I'm headed to Seattle now. I'm about an hour away."

"You're making the drive by yourself? Are you okay? You sound exhausted."

"I'm all right. It's just …" She paused, and for the first

time Elliot heard uncertainty in her voice. "It's just that maybe if you weren't too busy, I thought you could keep me company for a little bit." She laughed unconvincingly. "Sounds dumb when I put it that way."

"No," he interrupted. "I totally understand. I'm leaving the hospital now. I just finished my shift. Want me to come and meet you? We could drive the rest of the way together."

"No, you don't need to do anything like that. Could you stay on the line with me for a little bit?"

"Of course."

Any confusion he'd felt at how brusquely she'd ended the last call vanished. There was no way he wanted her alone at a time like this. He wished there was something more he could do.

"I'm so sorry about your friend." Was that the right thing to say? Maybe he should focus on something else, get her mind off her troubles.

Then again, hadn't it bothered him the way his friends stopped bringing Amy up after she died? Wasn't it better to talk through your worries than ignore them?

"Tell me about her." He hoped he wasn't making a mistake. "What's her name again? How long have you known each other?"

Ruby let out a little chuckle. "You got five or six hours?"

He turned back toward the sky bridge. "I've got all night."

CHAPTER 41

"So that was basically our first big fight. Pretty silly, huh?"

Ruby still couldn't believe how long she'd kept Elliot on the phone. When she called him up, she'd only wanted his ear for ten or fifteen minutes, enough to get her through the monotony of highway driving. Once she got into the city, she figured she'd let him go. But he'd asked about Jessi, and nearly an hour later she realized she'd said twenty or thirty words for every one of his.

"I'm so sorry. I've been talking your ear off. You're probably bored to death."

"No," he said and sounded sincere. Either he was a fabulous liar or a saint. "It was great hearing all about your antics. She sounds like a great best friend." There was something wistful in his voice.

"What about you?" she asked. She'd be at the hospital in ten minutes or less, but at least she could try to correct her mistake and let him do some of the talking for a change.

"Who was your best friend growing up?"

The line was quiet. What had she said wrong?

Elliot's voice was low. "I moved around a lot. Made it hard."

"That's too bad. Were you a military kid or something?"

Another awkward pause. "No. My grandma raised me until I was six, and then when she had a stroke, I got put in the foster system."

"Oh. That's too bad." What was she supposed to ask next? Well, she had to say something. He'd been so kind to keep talking to her on the phone for this long. "Umm, what was it like? The foster system I mean? Was it okay?"

"Sometimes." It was a cryptic answer, but she guessed from his tone it would probably be best to change the subject.

"Do you have any, like, brothers or sisters or anything?" She waited, hoping she hadn't made yet another conversational blunder. If she kept saying the wrong thing like this, there was no way he'd want to continue pursuing any sort of relationship.

"No," he answered, "no brothers or sisters."

Great. If her job was simply to make him miserable, she was achieving her goal with alarming success.

"But I'm back in touch with one of my foster sisters." This time there was a little more enthusiasm in his voice.

"That's great."

"Yeah, she's actually here in Seattle too. Maybe you could meet. You know, once things get settled down with your friend."

"That'd be nice." She was curious about siblings, about growing up in the foster system in general, but she'd have to wait until they got to know each other a little better before she jumped into all her questions.

"Well, I'm just about to the hospital now. Hey, can you tell me where to park? I don't know where the burn unit is."

"Yeah. You'll want to enter on the Lantern Street side. It's the smaller of the two entrances, the one across from a little park, and then I think it's the third floor that connects to the sky bridge. Hold on, how good are you with directions?

Ruby had to chuckle. Did he remember the story she'd just told him about how she'd gotten lost on the way from the library to her dorm room her first week of college and Jessi had to come and rescue her?

"Okay, how about this," Elliot went on. "What are you driving?"

She had no idea what that had to do with anything, but she told him anyway.

"What color? Is it blue?"

"Yeah." Lucky guess or did he remember seeing it in the Safe Anchorage driveway?

"Okay, are you at the stoplight now?"

"Yeah." Why did she feel like all of a sudden she'd been gifted her own personal stalker?

"Look over to the right and tell me what you see."

"A bus stop with a bunch of people."

"Go on."

"And some weird guy standing on the bench waving his arm … Oh. It's you."

She stared while Elliot hopped down and made his way to her car.

"Pull over, and let me in. I'll show you how to get there."

CHAPTER 42

If she'd known her drive to Seattle would end with Elliot Jameson sitting in her front seat, she would have made a little more effort to tidy up. At least she would have if this weren't such an emergency.

Elliot didn't say anything about the piles of wrappers, old text books, and empty soda cans by his feet while he gave her directions.

"I would have never been able to find this myself," Ruby admitted. "Did you even leave the hospital after you got out of work or have you just been hanging around here this whole time?"

They drove beneath a light in the garage, and she could see his dimpled grin. "I was just waiting around."

She was going to tease him for being silly but changed her mind. "Thanks. That was really sweet."

Another grin. "That's what I'm here for."

She tried to smile. Tried to forget for even a fraction of a second that somewhere nearby, her best friend was suffering.

Ruby parked the car, and Elliot led her down a maze of elevators, sky bridges, and hallways before they arrived at the burn unit.

"You go check on your friend," he told her, "and I'll wait over here."

She should give Mace a ring too. Wasn't he supposed to call after his nap? She'd text him as soon as someone here gave her some answers.

"I'm here to see Jessi Lacasa."

"Are you family?" the woman asked.

Ruby kept her voice down. "She's my sister-in-law." Hopefully the lie would be enough to bypass stupid patient privacy laws and let her see her friend.

The woman nodded without the slightest hint of a smile. "Come on back."

Ruby glanced back at Elliot, who was watching her the whole time. He gave her a nod, and she tried to return it with a smile.

The receptionist opened the door for her. "This way please."

Ruby took a deep breath and followed.

CHAPTER 43

Mace

I literally can't believe I fell asleep. I didn't mean to. I wasn't even pulled over when I told Ruby I was. Kept right on driving. But then I woke up to the sound of a horn blaring, and I guess I must have crossed into the wrong lane.

After getting off the phone with Ruby earlier, I told myself I'd go another five more minutes. If I didn't find some place to buy me some Rockstars or at least a Mountain Dew or something, I'd get to sleep. Next thing I know, I've got those headlights in my window. That's a way to get yourself alert when you're low on caffeine. So then I finally found a shoulder and parked. Probably smart of me. What wasn't smart was the way I forgot to set myself an alarm or anything.

Forty-five minutes later, I'm just now waking up. How stupid can I be? And the car's freezing. It's only fall, but it gets cold once the sun goes down.

I'm so stupid.

So here I am. I've been calling Ruby every minute or two, but she's not answering. Maybe that's good news. Maybe she's already there with Jessi, which means I'll get an update soon. I don't even have a phone number for the place where they're taking care of my sister.

I can't believe she went and got herself burned. And for those kids she doesn't even like. Maybe you'd think I wasn't paying attention in English 101, but I know what irony means.

I still can't believe it. I keep waiting for some director to turn on the overhead lights and shout "Cut!" and then my sister'll come out totally fine and laughing at me for being such an idiot for believing any part of the story.

"You know how much I hate those kids," she'll laugh. "I'd never do anything that stupid."

But you know what? I'm proud of her. Proud of the way she acted. Because I know the story's true. Jessi really did that, really went in to save that little boy stuck in the john. And I hate her for it because now I'm the one all worried, but I'm proud of her too.

My baby sis. A hero.

Who would've thought?

That's why I've been praying so hard. Telling God that

Jessi deserves to be healed. She deserves to be saved. Not the kind of saved like Ruby's been talking about where you ask God to come live in your heart. I just want to know my little sister's going to be all right.

I've been bargaining with God too. It sounds pretty stupid, but I find myself making him these deals. Like if he heals my sister, I'll start going to church. Not just once or twice a year either or even on all the major holidays. I'm talking every week.

If he makes Jessi okay, I'll pray every single day, and once I get me some kids, I'll take them to church and teach them their Sunday school stories and everything else.

The problem is it's hard to come up with the fine print. Know what I mean? Like what if Jessi doesn't die, but she's in the hospital for six months? Would I still have to hold up my end of the deal then?

What if she pulls through but they got to cut off her legs or something?

I don't want to hash out these little details. It doesn't seem right. So I've got to trust that when it happens, I'll know if my prayers have been answered good enough or not.

I guess it's probably not that uncommon for people to bargain with the Lord, but I'm not sure about threats. Yeah, I'm making some of those too.

I already told God what I'll do if he makes my sister better, so now I'm on to what I'll do if he doesn't.

Like I'll never believe in him at all even if that means I've got to give up my chances with Ruby.

I'll never set foot in church again, and I'll make sure Jessi doesn't have a service in a church either.

Funeral home's fine for her.

Sometimes I say these things, and I think to myself, *That'll show him.*

And other times I think he must be up there laughing because seriously, who can dream up with a threat strong enough to make God start to worry?

Know what I mean?

CHAPTER 44

Elliot was glad for the Kindle app on his phone. At least it gave him something to focus on. He'd purchased the book on genetically modified produce last month and was only now finding time to read it.

In between chapters, he texted Tiff a few times just to get his mind off everything. She offered a place at her home for Ruby to sleep, even though Tiff, her husband, and their baby were living in an apartment the size of Elliot's studio. But if Ruby didn't have any other options, it could work out at least short-term.

He thought about all they'd talked about so far, surprised by how little he really knew about her. She'd become a Christian after meeting Grandma Lucy, and Elliot himself was trying harder to return to the faith. He'd spent the first year or so after Amy died mad at God, but lately he'd been going to church with Tiff and her family. Praying more. Even reading his Bible.

It was a start.

Maybe Grandma Lucy had done something for both of them. Elliot hoped to find time to talk to Ruby about it. Most of the Christians he knew grew up in the church, and Elliot felt stupid asking them questions they probably hadn't wrestled with in years. But in some ways he and Ruby were both starting out in their faith, more or less on the same page. They could learn together.

Maybe when they went to Orchard Grove next weekend for that birthday party, he could ask Grandma Lucy if she had any good books to recommend, something to walk him through the early stages of the Christian life. Everyone had to start somewhere, right?

He glanced at the clock. It wasn't like he had anything pressing to be doing at home, so it was silly to feel this impatient. But he wondered how long Ruby would take, how broken she'd be when she came out.

More than anything, he hoped that God would use him tonight to be the encouragement she so clearly needed.

CHAPTER 45

Mace

Man, I could kill Ruby. Why doesn't she answer her stupid phone?

I'm finally caffeinated again. Got me some Rockstars and a few of those energy pills at a gas station a ways back. Ruby told me they're about the most dangerous thing you can do to your body, but I suppose falling asleep behind the wheel and getting yourself killed is even worse.

So I think I'm going to make it to Seattle tonight after all. I only wish Ruby'd pick up that blasted cell phone of hers and tell me what's going on with my sister.

The doctor or paramedic or whoever it was I was talking to at first told me to give him a ring if I had any questions. And at the beginning he was great about keeping me updated. He called when they got Jessi on the plane and when they landed in Seattle and when they got her checked into the burn center. Then he said just call if I had any more questions, only when I tried the number he dialed from, all I got was the automatic answering service for the entire hospital. Who's got time to listen to all those stupid numbers you're supposed to press to tell them who you want to talk to?

I don't even remember that stupid doctor's name.

The uncertainty is the worst. I swear it'll kill me if the caffeine overdose doesn't. But I'm done bargaining with God. I figure at this point he's either heard my prayers or he hasn't. He's either decided to heal my sister or not.

There's nothing I can do now but get to Seattle.

I'm going eighty or ninety most of the way. Stupid of me, I know, but you would too if it were your sister in the hospital. Man, I hate to think of what she looks like. Aren't burn patients all blistered and ugly? I mean, okay so maybe *ugly* isn't the right word. It's just if you knew my sister, you'd know she's totally wrapped up in herself. Literally. Like you know how some girls are into all that makeup and fingernails and toenails and beauty salons and shopping at malls and junk? That's my sis. She's always been like that. If she had her way, she'd be at the mall every single day, spending hundreds of dollars at the stores, but of course the daycare doesn't pay her enough for that to work out.

I'm so mad at that daycare joint. Did you know the boss

lady knew there might be a problem with the gas? But she left my sister there to heat up lunch for the kids while she ran off to take her own daughter to preschool. Yeah. Did I tell you that one? She doesn't even let her own daughter go to that miserable place. She takes her all the way across town to where some fancy lady in the Heights watches her from her home. Feeds the kids all that organic food junk instead of the canned stuff my sister heats up for all the ones who can't afford better.

I'm seriously glad that place is burned down, or I would have done it myself.

I'm glad the little ones are okay, though. Seriously. I'm not a monster. Nobody wants to see kids suffer.

Then again, nobody wants to see their sister suffer either, so there's that too.

But I'd like to go on record and say if I were to burn that joint to the ground, I would have been sure to do it after hours so nobody was hurt.

Man, I can't get over it. Making my sister use a bum stove …

It should be that boss lady in the burn unit. Maybe God'll punish me for saying so, but you can't really blame me for feeling that way. Not if you were to see how angry I am. My heart's pounding like I've been running laps all day. I'm sweating, I'm so mad and anxious. I can hardly think straight.

I'm a big mess.

Once I get closer to Seattle, I'll try to calm myself down. Clear my head a little. But right now, the rush is what's keeping me from falling asleep again at the wheel. It's what's allowing me to creep that dial up toward ninety-five whenever I get to a straight stretch of road.

It's the anger that's going to get me to my sister in time.

In time for what? That's what I don't know.

And if we're going to be totally honest, I'm not sure I want to.

CHAPTER 46

After an hour by Jessi's hospital bed, Ruby made her way back out to the waiting room. She hadn't cried at all. Did that make her a terrible person?

If Ruby had been the one all bandaged up with a breathing tube stuck down her throat, Jessi would have thrown herself on the hospital bed and sobbed enough tears to fill a small pool.

So why didn't Ruby feel anything?

Elliot was sitting in the lobby. She hadn't expected him to stay here the whole time. He glanced up from his phone.

Oh, no. Her cell. Had she left it in the car?

She needed to call Mace.

"Everything all right?" Elliot asked.

"Yeah, I mean, no. I mean, Jessi's okay. I was just back there."

Yes, Ruby would be this year's top choice for Captain Obvious.

She searched her pockets. "I need to call Jessi's brother."

She felt a slight flush in her cheeks when she glanced at Elliot. Was that because she hadn't mentioned the fact that she and Mace had dated for so many years? It wasn't like she'd kept it some big secret. They just hadn't gotten to that point in their conversation yet.

"I think I left my phone in the car."

He stood up. "Want to use mine?"

"I don't know his number."

"Okay. Let's go."

He was such a calming presence. Why was it that all of Ruby's closest friends, which basically just meant Jessi and her brother, were so high-strung and hyperactive? She had hardly spent any time with people like Elliot, people with soft-spoken voices, quiet manners …

She could get used to this.

"How's Jessi?" Elliot asked as they waited for their first elevator.

"They've got her sedated right now, which I guess is a good thing. They're mostly worried about infection."

He nodded. He knew way more medicine than she did, and they both understood how critical Jessi's condition would be over the next few days.

"I'm so sorry she's going through this. But that's really nice the nurse let you back there. I would have thought they'd only allow family."

The elevator door opened. Ruby shoved her hands into her pockets. "Yeah, about that, I kind of told them she was my sister-in-law." She glanced at him. Would he judge her for lying?

He smiled. "I've had patients do that sort of thing too. Once there was this patient, and her entire small group from church came over to pray with her, and they all told us they were her family. So it was like twenty people in the room, all colors and races, but none of us had the heart to do a single thing about it."

Her stomach flopped for a second when the elevator started moving. "Yeah, well, it's actually a little closer to the truth than maybe you'd expect."

He stared at her, confusion clear in his expression.

"See, you know that story I told you about how Jessi's brother got her to pretend to kidnap me just so he could be my rescuer and ask me to prom?"

"Yeah."

She kept her eyes focused on the elevator buttons. "Her brother and I dated for years. He's, um, he's really the only guy I've ever been with."

"Okay."

She lowered her voice. "I just wanted you to know

because he's on his way, and I didn't want things to get awkward or anything."

The elevator beeped, and the door opened. Was he going to say anything?

"That's totally fine. I mean, I'm glad you told me, and I can see why maybe you'd think I'd be worried, but it's no big deal. Are you uncomfortable being around him or anything?"

"What? No. He's like my brother. I couldn't imagine him not being here with me during all that's happening. I just …" She dared to raise her eyes to his. "I just don't want things to get weird."

He laughed. "All right. Here's the list of things that I think are weird. You ready?"

"Go for it."

"I'll think it's weird if you say that you're into shaving kittens and knitting socks with their fur. It's also weird if you tell me you have a pet boulder named Randy that you glued googly eyes onto and push around in a stroller. Those are the kinds of things I find weird. Your ex-boyfriend coming to Seattle because his sister is in the burn unit? Not weird."

She let out her breath. "Okay, thanks."

She tried to imagine how Mace would respond if their positions were reversed. Would he be anywhere near so composed?

It was strange to be close to a guy who wasn't always a little jealous. A little possessive.

Maybe her relationship with Mace had been even more off than she knew. It's not like she had any other experiences to compare it to.

She fell into a steady step beside Elliot, remembering how many times with Mace he'd walk so fast she'd have to nearly sprint to catch up.

Yeah, this was definitely something she could get used to.

CHAPTER 47

Elliot walked Ruby back to her car, thankful he'd decided to stay at the hospital to be with Ruby. He should have asked if she was hungry. The cafeteria wouldn't be serving any hot food at this time, but they could at least buy a fruit salad or something.

He'd ask her about that after she called Jessi's brother. And then he'd try to figure out where she could sleep. If nothing else worked, he could give her his place and he could spend the night with Tiff.

Ruby unlocked her car and gave him an uneasy glance. Why did she always look at him like that, like she was scared the littlest thing might make him mad?

What was this ex-boyfriend of hers like?

When she mentioned how long she'd dated Jessi's brother, Ruby acted as if that'd somehow be this major deal breaker. As if Elliot would throw a fit to think that she'd dated someone else in the past. Seeing how nervous she was mentioning him, he wondered what kind of guy he was.

Ruby glanced up at him.

"Your phone in there?" he asked.

"Yeah, it's here. It's just …" She bit her lip. "Do you mind if I …" She pointed to the door of the car.

"You want a little privacy? Sure. Take all the time you need."

She looked at him as if he'd just agreed to give her one of his kidneys. "Thanks." Relief washed over her face.

Elliot hadn't done much exercising today other than the walking that came natural to him during his rounds. "I'll wait over here," he told her and found a spot by a pillar where he didn't have to worry about a car running him over while he stretched.

He wasn't sure if Ruby would take two minutes or twenty or maybe even more, so however long he had to wait, he might as well make the best use of his time as possible.

CHAPTER 48

"Mace, can you hear me?" Ruby strained her ears. He must be driving through a bad reception area. "Mace?"

"I'm here. Why didn't you call?"

"I'm sorry." She'd grabbed her cell to find over twenty messages and texts. "I left my phone in the car."

"So you're there? You're with Jessi?"

"Well, I'm at the hospital. I'm not with her anymore, but I just came back from her room."

"How is she?"

A few hours ago when they talked, Mace sounded as if he were mumbling in his sleep. Now he was as animated as those nights when he got himself a new video game to try out.

"She's doing okay." Ruby wondered how much she should reveal. Mace had to be prepared for when he got to his sister's room and saw all those bandages, those tubes. But she didn't want to scare him with a lot of medical jargon either. "She's stable now. It's just that …"

"What's wrong with her? I want you to tell me everything. I'm ready. I can handle it."

She sighed. Just talking to him made her blood pressure rise. "Right now, she's okay. She's not in any pain …"

"Why not? Is she all drugged up? What did she say? Did you tell her I'm coming?"

"She's in a …." Ruby stopped herself before using the word *coma*, a word that would definitely tip Mace into freak-out mode if he weren't already there. "She's got anesthesia so she doesn't feel the pain."

"Isn't that what they give patients for surgeries? Isn't that how it works? Did they do a surgery? Are they going to have to amputate or anything?"

Ruby sometimes forgot how similar he and his sister really were.

"Right now, she's fine," Ruby assured him. "She's comfortable. She's not in any pain. There's a lot of bandages, though. She'll look different to you."

"Different like what? You know how stuck-up she gets about her looks. Is she scarred or anything? What'd she say about the fire? Is all the attention going to her head?"

"I don't know about that part." Ruby had to think fast. The last thing she needed was for Mace to get so upset he got himself into an accident.

"What do you mean? Weren't you just there? Didn't you talk to her?"

"She was really tired." There. That part was the truth. Basically. "She was tired, and she's got a tube that makes it hard to say anything …" She winced, waiting for his response.

"A tube? What are you talking about? Like, is that how they're feeding her or something?"

Ruby was certain that giving Jessi a full-course meal was the lowest priority on any of her doctors' or nurses' lists.

"Just a tube to help her breathe." Since it'd still be there when he arrived, he may as well start getting used to the idea. She knew Mace well enough to know that he needed plenty of time to warm up to bad news.

"But she doesn't hurt? Can she write? Can she use sign language or something?"

Ruby sighed. This was going about as well as she'd feared.

"Just don't get your hopes up too high when you get here, okay?"

"What's that mean? Is that what she told you to tell me? Does she assume I can't handle it? She's probably thinking about when she got that big gash on her leg from falling out of a tree, remember that? I didn't do so well when she needed those stitches, but I was only thirteen or fourteen. It's different now. I can handle it."

Ruby made her voice sound as gentle as possible. "I'm sure you can. I just want you to be prepared."

"I am," he assured her, and Ruby shook her head, knowing it wasn't true.

CHAPTER 49

She got out of the car and looked around for Elliot. Where did he go?

"Over here."

She turned, and there he was, doing standing push-ups against one of the parking garage's cement pillars.

He righted himself and walked toward her. "Everything okay?"

"Yeah. Mace'll be here in about half an hour."

"Good."

"Well, I just wanted to thank you for spending the extra time with me here tonight. It was really sweet of you."

To be honest, she hadn't even expected him to still be hanging around when she finished visiting Jessi.

He hesitated, and she glanced around the parking garage before finally asking, "Can I give you a lift to your car or something?"

"Oh." He seemed surprised at the suggestion but quickly recovered. "No, that's fine. So you're good? I thought maybe you'd want to grab a bite to eat."

She shook her head. There was no way she'd have an appetite after a day like this. Visions of her best friend lying there, so broken, so helpless … "No, I'm not hungry." She smiled and tried to soften her voice. "But thanks for asking."

Was he disappointed?

She took a step toward the exit that would lead her back to the sky bridge. "I should go. But thanks again. It's been …" She turned around and offered what would likely go down in history as the most awkward hug ever. "It's been really nice. Having you around and all."

Great. Her vocabulary had diminished to that of a second-grader. Oh, well. At least he knew what he'd be getting into if he decided to pursue this relationship further.

She didn't look back. His goodbye rang in her ears and echoed in the parking structure as she made her way back to the burn unit.

CHAPTER 50

"No, it was good. It just …" Elliot sighed as he paced the floor in his apartment. All twelve feet of it. "It ended kind of fast."

On the other end of the line, he heard Tiff's baby cough.

"Hold on a minute," Tiff said. "Jake's at work, and I've gotta turn on this suction machine."

There was a loud whir, the coughing stopped, and his foster sister was back on the line.

"So it was good though? You think you guys are hitting it off pretty well?"

"Yeah, I mean, it's terrible what's happened to her friend. Honestly, I'm mostly worried about making sure she's got a place to stay and food to eat."

"You're such a goody goody."

Elliot wasn't entirely sure if he should take her words as a compliment or an insult.

"Seriously," she went on. "I mean, you're like literally the nicest guy I know. I teased you to death when we were at the same foster home. I hid your inhaler in a box of tampons for crying out loud. And you're still this amazing, huggable, forgiving sweetheart and the best uncle to Natalie, and I'm serious when I say you deserve every single bit of happiness this girl can bring your way. If she's the right one, of course." Her tone got serious. "And if she's not, I'll give her a good dose of Tiff's special if she even thinks about breaking that soft little heart of yours."

Elliot couldn't keep from smiling. "Thanks. I think."

"You're welcome. I think." Tiff chuckled. "Come on. You're like Seattle's most eligible bachelor. If she can't see that, she's too dumb for you to begin with."

"I think you might be exaggerating a little …"

"Pfft. Come on. What's not to love about you? Honestly? You're kind-hearted, super brainy, good with kids. You drive the sweetest car in town, you're filthy rich, or at least you will be once you start your own practice and pay off your school loans. And any time there's a medical emergency, you're right there. You're literally the best package on the market right now."

It was sweet of Tiff to give him this pep talk, even if he didn't deserve half of her praise.

"So anyway," she went on, "you just tell her that if she needs a place to stay, she can come over here. I don't know what it's like to have a friend in a burn unit, but I've spent however many months now in and out of the hospital with Natalie, so I'm sure the two of us could swap stories. And if she wants time alone, which makes perfect sense and is totally fine too, then she can stay at your place and you can crash here."

"Yeah. We'll see."

"What do you mean *we'll see*?" Tiff was like a shark. She could sniff out weakness or hesitation from miles away.

"Well, there's still that other guy. You know, her friend's brother."

"What, the ex-boyfriend? What's he got on you? Didn't Ruby say he was like some dope-head drop-out or something?"

"It's not that bad."

"Well, does he have his medical degree? Is he on the fast track to becoming one of Seattle's most sought-after oncologists? Does he have the slickest ride in the western half of the state? Does he wake up and drink raw kale every morning? I think not. You don't have any reason to feel threatened."

"Who's feeling threatened?" Elliot asked. "I was just mentioning him because he's obviously going to need a place to stay if Ruby does, right?"

"Oh. Yeah."

"So what great wisdom do you have about that?" Elliot asked.

Tiff thought. "Umm, I guess he could stay over here and …"

"So where's that leave Ruby? And if Jake's working nights do you seriously think I'm going to let you open up your home to a perfect stranger?"

"What about Ruby?" Tiff remarked. "She's a stranger. And with as much as you've been gushing over her, she sounds pretty perfect."

"You know what I mean."

"Oh, I do? Is what you're saying that you're totally fine offering my home to some woman I don't know from Adam, but when we start talking about a guy, it's totally different?"

"It is totally different."

Tiff didn't argue.

"So what do we do?" Elliot finally asked.

"Maybe he could stay at the Ronald McDonald House."

"Or I could have him over here and send Ruby to sleep with you."

"Oh, that's perfect." Tiff chuckled. "Invite your rival over so you can find out what you're up against?"

"You don't know what you're talking about."

She laughed again. "Right. And our foster mother was skinny as a supermodel."

Elliot smiled. He and Tiff had spent a decent amount of time talking about their past, but she remembered a whole lot more details than he did.

"So what are you going to do, genius?" she finally asked.

"I don't know. I guess I'll get the place tidied up, and if they both need a place to crash, they can do it here."

Through Tiff's silence, he could almost see her dubious expression.

"What? What's wrong?"

"I didn't say anything."

"What is it?" he pressed.

"Nothing. If you think it's a good idea."

"What's wrong with the idea?"

"Drop it. Just call to let me know if you or anyone else is going to need my couch. And warn whoever's coming the place is a mess. But they're welcome to the couch, and I even have a sleeping bag. So call me, but try to figure it all out before too long, okay? I think Natalie's about to go to sleep, and I'm about to crash too. I've been awake for like twenty hours already. I hate when Jake works nights."

"All right. I'll be in touch soon. Otherwise I'll just chat with you in the morning."

"Okay," Tiff answered. "Remember that no matter how much history she and this childhood sweetie of hers might share, you're the one she's after now. This is your time. I swear you've waited long enough."

"Thanks, Tiff. I really appreciate all you've done."

He could practically hear her eyes rolling in their sockets. "Don't get mushy. Please. I'm way too tired for that."

"Fine. But let me thank you properly. You're an amazing sister."

The word hung in the air between them. Had he ever called her that before?

If you were to stand the two of them together, there's no way you'd think they were related. Tiff was dark-skinned with a whole head of black, wiry curls. And even though she was kind and encouraging and his biggest cheerleader, she still looked as tough as the girl who'd stolen Elliot's inhaler when they lived together as kids.

Elliot started his adult life at a disadvantage because of his childhood, but Tiff was African-American and a woman as well as one of the unfortunate souls to age out of the foster program. She'd earned every single ounce of toughness she had.

But she could be as soft as velvet with the people she

loved.

The people she considered family.

Which is why Elliot had used that word.

She called him Uncle Elly when her daughter was around, but this was different.

Had he crossed a line?

"You're not too bad yourself, bro."

A smile spread across his face, but by the time he thought of something to say that wasn't too cheesy, Tiff had already ended the call.

CHAPTER 51

Ruby was restless. There wasn't a single magazine in the tiny sitting room she cared to read, and even being that close to the doctors and nurses coming in and out of the burn unit was enough to remind her of how bad off Jessi was.

She'd lost track of how long she'd been pacing the hallways up and down. Sometimes she felt like she was the only soul here who had a loved one close to death, but that was ridiculous.

So why did she feel so alone?

Her mind recited all the reasons Jessi couldn't die. Hadn't they both sworn to be each other's maids of honor at their weddings? Hadn't they both dreamed about raising children together, growing old together?

They had laid out their future more comprehensively than most couples plan their marriage. Once they both got their finances in order, Ruby and Jessi were going to take some kind of wild vacation together at least twice a year. Cruises, day trips to amusement parks, train rides across the country.

Ruby and Jessi both promised they wouldn't marry anyone who would even think about separating them. Military men were out of the running. As was anybody who had any ambitions to one day leave Washington state.

She shook her head. How old had they been when they first pinky-promised to be best friends forever? Aside from that one fight in tenth grade, they literally hadn't gone more than two days without talking. The one semester that Jessi stayed in college and Ruby went back home to take care of her mom, they added up all their phone minutes and in a month had talked for over sixty-five hours.

That didn't even count their texts or weekend visits.

The truth was Ruby didn't even know who she was without Jessi.

Her eyes welled up with tears. Stupid emotions. Couldn't she just turn them off? The doctors had been merciful enough to put Jessi in a coma during the worst of the pain. Couldn't they do the same for her?

Footsteps rushed up behind her.

"Rubes?"

She was too tired to even run to him but simply held out her hands.

Mace was hugging her, and in a few seconds, she was

crying into his chest.

"Is she okay?" he kept repeating. "My sister, is she okay?"

How was Ruby supposed to respond? No. Jessi wasn't okay. She might never be okay.

None of this made sense. None of this was right.

Why Jessi? Why not someone else? If God had felt so compelled to let someone burn in that fire today, why did he have to pick the most important person in Ruby's life?

Her tears were doing nothing to soothe her spirit, and they were freaking Mace out. He probably thought his sister had died in the past few minutes between when they last talked and now.

"Can we go see her?" he asked. "I've got to talk to her."

"She can't talk." It was time for Mace to get his full dose of reality.

"You already told me about that tube. But she can do something. Write a letter, nod her head."

"She's asleep."

"So I'll wake her up. You know how ticklish she is."

It was more than Ruby could handle. "Stop it. Just stop." She was pacing again. Thankfully he stayed in one place and didn't try to follow her around. She had to make him understand. "The burns are bad. She's covered in bandages, head to foot. Literally. And I'm talking about that word in its correct context, not how you're always using it."

He blinked, then stared at her.

She shook her head. She'd lost him with the grammar lesson. Time to backtrack. "She has a tube down her throat to help her breathe. If she were awake, it would keep her from talking, but that's not an issue right now because she's heavily sedated."

"What, like drugged up?" The lights were starting to go on. Slowly but surely. He was beginning to understand.

"The good news is she can't feel anything. She's not uncomfortable at all." Ruby hoped that was right and not just something doctors and nurses said to make people feel better. It wasn't like you could ask a coma patient if they were in pain.

More often than not, having a medical background was a curse rather than a blessing.

She sniffed and dried her eyes. "You can go in there, but you have to check with the nurse first. They'll make you wear special clothes, and you can't touch her. At all."

"Why not?"

"Because they're worried about an infection. With the burns covering her …" She stopped. He didn't need a science lecture. "Without the …" What was she saying? She squeezed her eyes shut for a moment. *Because if she gets an infection she'll die,* she wanted to scream at him.

Instead, she took a deep breath in. "Because the doctors need to be very careful to keep her burns free of any germs. Got it?"

"Okay." He nodded his head once. "That's it?"

She stared at him. Had he heard a single word she said? Had he taken any of it in?

"Yeah, I guess that's it."

"All right, well thanks for filling me in. Now where can I go see my sister?"

CHAPTER 52

Mace

I'm here, but I'm not here. It's kind of trippy that way. Once I told the lady behind the desk who I was, they let me back. Had this whole long session about what I could or couldn't do, wanted to know if I'm the closest kin, and before you know it we were talking about paperwork and insurance and junk like that.

Finally I had to tell her, "Listen lady, I'm her brother. I don't know anything else about anything. I'm just here because I want to see my sister. Can we do that?"

And she nodded.

I guess that Mace charm can still work its magic.

You should have seen Ruby a few minutes ago, holding on to me, sobbing her eyes out. She's a big mess. I didn't want to tell her, but her makeup was running like crazy. Jessi would tease her endlessly if she could see.

There I go again. I swear it's like my brain doesn't even

fully realize what's going on. Sometimes I find myself saying something like, *When I get back, I'm going to have to tell Jessi about* ... just as if I'm on some field trip and am here to see the sights before I go home where my sister really is.

I'm still mad at myself for going back to Spokane. Jessi and I were just together. I mean, seriously, if I'd been there, if I'd stayed in Orchard Grove …

Then what? I might have magically been passing by that daycare and could have run in to save that boy on the pot so she didn't have to? Then I'd be the one all drugged up and bandaged like a mummy with tubes shoved down my throat.

I'd take it.

Did you hear me, God? I said I'd take it. I'd trade spots with her in a heartbeat.

Wouldn't even have to think about it.

She looks so tiny. I mean, she's always been skinny. Kind of stuck-up about it too, the sort of girl who makes fun of the heavy ones no matter what people are saying nowadays about the evils of fat-shaming. I guess I've done that too though, so I'm not really one to talk.

She's always been proud of her looks, and I know guys notice her even though I have no idea what they see in my little sis, but now you couldn't even tell if she were a man or woman. I guess if she were a man, she'd be a pretty small one, but literally her eyes and a little bit around her lips are all you can see of her.

Why didn't Ruby warn me?

I wasn't ready for this.

I'll never be ready for this.

You hear that, God? This isn't what I signed up for. I thought I told you that if you wanted me to believe in you, you were going to have to heal my sister. I didn't know what that would exactly look like, but this sure isn't it.

She's not even awake. The nurse was trying to tell me, something about her going into a coma … I can't handle it. I can only stay here a minute or two. Then I tell her I'm ready to go.

"You sure?" she asks me, and I don't care if it makes me look like I'm the most deadbeat brother on the face of the planet. I'm not spending another second in this room.

Know why? Because I figured something out.

That mummy, that thing they've got all wrapped up in blankets? That's not even Jessi. They've got it all wrong. Someone else ran into the daycare and went after that boy. My sister, she's too selfish and too conceited about her looks to ever do something like that.

It's a mix-up. That's all.

Whoever it was, whatever superhero stranger dashed in to save that boy on his flaming toilet or whatever, it was someone else, but they were so badly injured people couldn't tell who it was, so they just assumed it must be my sister.

Meanwhile, Jessi's probably hiding out at home, reading all these reports about how heroic she is, and I'm sure she's laughing it up. Day or two she'll let us all know it was one big practical joke, and we'll all laugh.

All of us except the mummy on the hospital bed.

I don't even look back. I don't care who it is. I've seen enough to know it's not Jessi, and that's all I need.

I'm outta here.

And not a second too soon.

CHAPTER 53

Ruby stood up from her chair when Mace came back out. "You okay?" she asked.

He didn't even look at her. Just made a mad dash around the corner. She heard him heaving into a trash can before she even found where he was.

"Mace?" She put her arm on his shoulder, and he jerked back at the touch.

"Mace?"

Tears streamed down from his eyes. He shook his head, then leaned down and retched again.

A nurse in polka dots walked by and handed Ruby some paper towels. Didn't say another word, like this sort of thing happened here all the time.

Ruby bit her lip.

"Mace?"

He wasn't ready yet. She handed him the paper towels, glanced around for a bathroom sign, and hurried away.

Man, she looked awful. It would have been infinitely

better if she'd never put makeup on today.

The water she splashed onto her face was cold and had some sort of rusty, metallic smell.

Gross.

The paper towels were coarse, but who was she to complain about a little irritated skin when her best friend …

She understood why Mace was reacting the way he was.

In fact, Ruby was surprised that she hadn't broken down herself. There were a few tears when Mace got there, but that was because she'd been so worried about how he'd respond to seeing Jessi.

God, what are we supposed to do now?

She'd already called Connie, told her she'd be in Seattle at least through the week. She didn't even know where she'd stay. She'd curl up in a chair in the lobby and sleep there if she had to.

But now Mace was here, and she felt responsible to take care of him too.

It wasn't fair. He was older. How often had he bragged that he was the most mature out of the three of them? And he couldn't even sit in that room five minutes with his sister.

Sympathy morphed seamlessly to anger.

Not just anger.

Hot rage.

Hot as the fire that burned her friend.

Mace was a wreck. He needed to get control of his emotions, accept reality, and make some decisions for a change.

She wasn't even his girlfriend anymore. It wasn't up to her to figure out where they'd sleep, what they'd eat, who'd stay in the room in case Jessi woke up and needed anything.

She was Jessi's best friend, but he was her brother for crying out loud.

Had he thought through anything when he hopped into his car to drive all the way out here? No. And she knew with absolutely certainty that the only reason he hadn't asked himself those kinds of questions was because he assumed Ruby would be the one to make all those arrangements.

Ruby would pick up all the pieces of his messed up life and fix it all up for him. Like always. Would he even have made it to his sixth year of college if it hadn't been for her?

What about that terrible essay she'd completely rewritten for him about the French Revolution? What about all those nights she'd spent practically doing his homework for him so he could pass college algebra?

How many years had she wasted with this child of a man, a child who couldn't even hold himself together long enough to be there for his sister when she needed it?

Hot tears streamed down her cheeks, but she didn't care. It was better to be angry at Mace, infinitely better, than to face her fears and sorrows over what happened to Jessi.

She'd fight with Mace every single day, every single minute of her life if it could keep her mind free from the sorrow that threatened to drown her. She splashed more of that stupid, rusty water on her face, hating the way it burned her nostrils. Hating the way she had to either choose hatred or grief.

Hating the way that when Mace walked into the bathroom, looking sheepish and still smelling like vomit, she threw herself into his arms and prayed she would never have to let go.

CHAPTER 54

Mace

Maybe it's because Ruby is the only girl I've ever dated for real, but I'm not sure how good I am at reading women. See, one minute Ruby sees me in the bathroom — I just came in here to check on her because even from outside I could hear her sobbing — and she's holding onto me like I'm Jesus himself.

Next minute, she's pounding me with her fists, telling me I'm a man-child and I've wasted her life and she never wants to see me again.

If I had to make a guess, I'd say that it has something to do with the way I couldn't spend more than a couple minutes with Jessi. I guess Ruby was different and stayed in there close to an hour. At least that's what she tells me, and knowing her, I'm surprised it wasn't longer.

But I'm not strong like Ruby. I never have been. That's why we're so good for each other.

What's that complex people get when all they want to do

is fix, fix, fix and heal, heal, heal? That's what Ruby's got. Why else would she have become a nurse, right?

She's just one of those people who always needs someone to take care of. Couple years ago, she had her mom to look out for, but now her mom's gone.

So that leaves me.

I thought we had a great arrangement. Ruby's the kind of person who always wants someone to help. I'm the kind of person who's happy to let other people take care of me.

You should have seen her when I showed her the essay I wrote about some big war in Europe a while back. She literally rewrote the entire thing for me. Got me an A, but that's not the point. The point is that if she didn't have me to take care of and worry over, she'd just go find someone else. I swear that's why she's working for that Grandma Lucy lady. From what I hear from Jessi, the woman's off her rocker big time, but she'll have a good day every now and then, so nobody wants to admit how bad it's really gotten.

Anyway, Ruby and me are perfect for each other. Always have been. Except this is new. Her getting mad at me. As if it was my fault I love my sister so much I had to leave her alone.

You should hear all the names she's calling me. Apparently, I'm selfish, pig-headed, stubborn, egotistical, immature, and I'm still stuck in early adolescence. I thought that one was pretty clever myself.

I don't usually take a beating from nobody, but I figure maybe this is her way of expressing her anger. See, I didn't pass psychology 101 for nothing. She's hurting over Jessi just as much as I am, and she's probably mad it took me longer to get here because I had to stop and take that stupid nap.

So I'll take her shouts and her fists, and I'll have forgotten about it by morning, I'm sure. That's how things always work out between me and Ruby, you know. We fight, swear we never want to see each other again, and by the next day we're totally fine. Water off a duck's back or however that saying goes.

She's telling me I'm the biggest mistake she ever made, but I know she doesn't mean it. That's the grief talking. My psych professor would be proud of me.

So I let her yell, and I tell myself tomorrow's a new day, and we'll start over fresh.

Because that's what we do.

Ruby's my girl, and I'm her man.

And no matter what anybody else has to say about it, that's the way it's going to be.

Always.

CHAPTER 55

It took all her energy, but Ruby finally managed to throw Mace out of the bathroom while she cleaned herself up. She hadn't meant to lose her temper at him. Not here. Not like that.

But it was just as well. That boy had to grow up sometime. With his sister in the burn ward and not even guaranteed to survive the night, it may as well be now.

Her phone beeped. Good. She'd take any excuse she could get to wait in here before she had to face Mace again. What was he doing, stomping into the women's bathroom like that in the first place?

She glanced at her message.

You need a place to stay for the night? I can help you find a room.

Elliot was so thoughtful. If she had met someone like him years ago, maybe she would have realized how pathetic her relationship with Mace had grown. Maybe she and Mace were good for each other when they were teens without any cares or responsibilities, but he never grew up, and she wasn't going to wait another ten or fifteen years for him to mature.

If he ever did.

That's really nice of you, she wrote back. *I'm not quite sure what we're doing yet.*

She stared at the screen and erased the last sentence.

Not sure what I'm doing yet.

That was better.

She took a deep breath. Why did her throat hurt? Was it from screaming at Mace, or was she hurting vicariously after seeing Jessi intubated?

Her skin was starting to itch. Had she overheated from yelling, or were those sympathy pains too?

She remembered her nursing school rotation in the burn unit so clearly. Everyone told her there was nothing more painful for a human being than to recover from full-body burns.

She and her classmates were toward the end of their training by then, but several of her fellow students had reacted just as viscerally as Mace.

She couldn't do this anymore. Couldn't keep worrying about him when it took all her energy to hold herself together. Keep her sanity. Try to survive all this stress without giving herself a heart attack.

He needed to grow up. He'd have to figure some things out for himself.

Like whether he was going to be a big boy and stay here for his sister, or whether he was going to run back home because he didn't have the stomach for it.

Maybe she should be more compassionate. She'd certainly dealt with patients as queasy as he was, and she'd been gentle and professional with each and every one.

But this was different. She was just so tired of his immaturity. And she wasn't the only one who was suffering. If he abandoned his sister here at this hospital, Ruby would never speak to him again.

Period.

I can crash at my sister's and let you sleep in my place. It's small, but it's close to the hospital.

She read Elliot's text and sighed. He was so kind to take that much time out of his day to make sure she was all right. She didn't know what time he usually went to bed, but with the hours he worked, she figured she'd kept him up far too late already.

That's sweet, she wrote back, *but I really don't want to inconvenience you.*

Then again, what other choice did she have? She'd been

so mad at Mace for refusing to think things through, but the truth was she hadn't either.

She paused with her fingers above her screen. Was she going to take this chance?

Maybe it was time to let someone else take care of her for a change.

But I don't really know what else to do, so I'd really appreciate it.

She reread her message and added a quick *if you're sure it's not too much hassle,* keeping all the typos in her rush.

She let out her breath.

So she had a place to sleep.

Now it was time to go break the news to Mace.

Before she left the bathroom, she splashed some more water on her face.

She needed all her mental energy.

CHAPTER 56

Mace

It's like I don't even know who she is anymore.

Rubes, is that you? I want to knock on her forehead and see if some alien opens a trapdoor into her brain.

"I still don't get it," I tell her.

She huffs, all impatient. "What's not to get? I have a place to stay for the night, so I'm going there. I'll see you in the morning."

"You're leaving me here?" Somewhere in the back of my brain I'm sure there's a simple explanation for why she's acting like this, but I swear I have no idea what it is.

"Yes. I'm leaving you here. Have you been listening to what I've said?"

Well, it's fine that Miss Smarty Pants has a place lined up to sleep, but that still doesn't tell me where I'm supposed to go. "What about me?"

Any minute, I expect her to laugh and grin and tell me,

"I'm just kidding around. Come on. I found us a place for the night. Let's go."

But she doesn't.

Wait a minute. I know what's going on.

"Is this because of your whole no sleeping together before we're married thing?" If she seriously thinks I'd feel up for anything like that the day my sister nearly died, she's an even bigger idiot than any sixth-year college student in the country.

She shakes her head and looks at me like she's disgusted. "No. This is because it's late, and I'm tired."

"I thought we'd figure out something together."

Is she seriously going to roll her eyes at me now after trying to beat me up in the bathroom? "You thought wrong."

That's it? That's literally all she has to say? After I drove all this way …

"Why are you acting like this?" I have a suspicion of my own, but I don't want to say anything until I'm more sure.

"Acting like what?" Well, doesn't she sound all testy.

"Like you don't even want to be with me. Like you can't stand the sight of me."

Ruby and me have had more arguments than I eat pizza in a year, but she's never looked at me like that before.

Like I'm disgusting to her.

She puts her hands up to her head like she's trying to keep her brain from popping out of her eyes. "Listen, I'm tired. I've been driving forever, and I'm worried sick about your sister."

She says the *your* like I'm in some sort of trouble. Like I'm the one who didn't fix that stupid gas leak that blew Jessi up.

"We have a lot to talk about," she says, and for the first time all night I agree with her. "But it's all going to have to wait," she finishes, and all of a sudden, I'm watching her walk away and leave me all alone.

CHAPTER 57

"Wow. Sweet ride." Ruby smiled as she got into Elliot's sports car. "You didn't have to pick me up, you know. Don't you have to be up crazy early?"

He shrugged, and Ruby wondered how he could be so nice to her and still make it seem like she was the one doing him some big favor.

"I didn't want you to get lost," he said.

With as directionally challenged as Ruby was, it was probably a good thing. She'd never have found his place on her own.

And it was nice to have a little bit of extra time together. Just being with Elliot made her feel calmer. More like herself.

How was it that some people could make her feel so anxious and stressed, and others could bring her peace of mind just by being in close proximity?

"Any changes in Jessi's condition?" he asked.

Ruby shook her head. "I got a quick update from the

nurse. Her temperature's up. They're a little worried about whether or not her heart can withstand the intensity of it all."

It was refreshing to speak to someone who already understood the mechanics and physiology behind Jessi's injuries. Nice not to have to dumb it all down.

As far as burn victims went, Jessi was young and healthy, but still …

Elliot didn't try to say anything stupid like "I'm sure she'll be fine," and they drove the last few blocks in silence.

He really hadn't been joking when he said his apartment was close to the hospital.

He led her up an outdoor staircase. "I'm warning you, it's not much."

He wasn't making an understatement. There was a small futon couch with a black mattress, two long windows with potted plants lining both walls, a kitchen area large enough for a dorm-size fridge and a two-burner stove, and a small chair and folding table in the corner.

"Wow." She hoped he didn't hear her. She wasn't trying to be rude.

"Yeah, it's pretty simple."

She turned to him. Was he actually blushing?

He pulled his keys out of his pocket. "So, um, I'd show you around, but it's kind of all here. Is there anything else you think you'll need? Want me to ask Tiff if she's got any clothes you can borrow in the morning?"

"That'd be great." She paused. "Are you sure you're okay with this? Giving up your room?"

"Yeah. I mean, Tiff's a night owl, and she's always complaining we don't spend enough time together and ..." He stopped himself and took a step toward her.

"I really want to help out."

"Why?" It was stupid for her to ask, but now that she had she was dying to know the answer. She couldn't remember the last time someone had shown her so much kindness without expecting anything in return.

"You want the long explanation or the short one?" he asked with a beginning trace of a grin. Man, he was handsome when he smiled.

She glanced at the clock. "Somewhere in between?"

He chuckled. "Okay. I want to help because nobody should have to watch someone they care about so deeply suffering that much. And ever since the woman I was treating got healed, I've been looking for ways to show God how much I appreciate all he's done. And ..." He lowered his eyes.

Now she was certain he was blushing.

"And I really care about you. I'd like to say I'd do this

for anyone, but the truth of the matter is I'm a little bit fond of my futon."

They both chuckled.

"It feels good to know that I can do something to help you out. To take care of you. Man, I hope that didn't sound condescending."

She stepped toward him, and for the first time she remembered that night in his dark office without wanting to die of mortification.

He was a great kisser if she remembered right.

But maybe she needed a little refresher.

He stepped back, holding his keys up like a shield. "I need to go." That crooked smile of his was almost too much to take in. "Seriously."

She nodded. He was right.

He looked down at her with such open admiration in his expression she could hardly catch her breath.

"See you in the morning," he whispered.

"Yeah, see you," she said when she finally found her voice, but by then he was already gone.

CHAPTER 58

"So, how's Miss Perfect?" Tiff asked, chomping on some Oreos.

Elliot had figured his foster sister would have the munchies and brought along some trail mix so they could have a late-night snack together.

"She's all right," he answered. "It's been a hard day."

"Yeah." Tiff looked out the window sadly. Elliot wondered if she was remembering when her daughter was born, the start of all those hospital stays.

He tried to change the subject. "How are you and Jake doing? Things still going well?

She nodded. "Yeah. We've been going to this couple's class at church, the one I was telling you about last week, and it's giving us some really good information. I'm serious. They should make people go through that sort of stuff before they even think about getting married." Tiff threw a whole Oreo into her mouth. "So tell me more about this Ruby girl who's got your heart all aflutter."

"Well, she's a nurse. I'm sure I mentioned that part before."

"No," Tiff said with her mouth full. "I didn't ask what she does. You need to describe her to me."

"Okay." He thought. Where should he even begin? "She's got dark hair, not quite black but pretty close to it. She wears it kind of long …"

"Not what she looks like." Tiff huffed and donned her well-practiced *men are such idiots* expression. "Just tell me about her personality. What are her interests, her hobbies, things like that?"

He thought back over all he knew. "To be totally honest, I'm not a hundred percent sure."

"Didn't you say about anything to each other all night?" Tiff demanded.

"Yeah."

She drank her cup of milk in just a few gulps. "So, what all did you talk about?"

"Mostly about Jessi."

"You didn't learn a single thing about her?"

"Just how much she loves her best friend. And how they got in huge trouble one year at summer camp when they snuck out to go swimming on the lake. And how on the night of their prom they both tried this pimple cream that gave them huge rashes. And in college they …"

Tiff chuckled. "Are they best friends, or are they married?"

He laughed too, but then Tiff got serious.

"It must be really hard for her. With her friend so hurt."

"Yeah, burn injuries are basically the worst, at least when you're talking about the pain level and recovery time."

Great. When had their conversation turned so depressing?

"I can tell you really care about her." Tiff was smiling at him with an almost maternal gaze. He'd never seen her look at anyone but her daughter that way.

Elliot was thankful for one person he could be totally honest with. "I do. I care a lot."

"I'm glad. I know how hard it was for you losing your fiancée. I'm just happy to see you're not letting that stop you from going out and living again."

He nodded. "It's what she wanted me to do."

Tiff was one of the only people who knew about his last conversation with Amy the night she died.

She sighed. "Well, I really do need to try to get some sleep. What time do you need to wake up in the morning?"

He stood. "I should be out of here by five at the latest."

"You're serious?"

"Yeah. I've got to be to work by six, and I'll be riding my bike. I told Ruby I'd leave her the car so she can get herself to the hospital when she's ready."

Tiff's eyes widened. "You're letting her drive the Tesla? She must be even prettier than I thought."

He didn't respond, and Tiff shrugged. "Well, don't wake her up that early if you can help it. I think you should let her sleep." She waved her hand in the air dismissively. "It's late. You know where everything is. Make yourself at home. Jake's not off until six, so lock the door behind you in the morning."

"I will. Thanks again for letting me stay here. Hey, is there anything Natalie needs during the night? Any way I can help?"

She shook her head. "We're doing her tube feeds only during the day now, and with the new seizure meds she's on, once she gets to sleep, she's pretty much out for the night. It's getting her to go down that's hard, but you missed all that part."

"Okay," he said. "Go get some sleep, and I'll see you later."

"Yeah," she mumbled, "I hope it's not at five in the morning, because I intend to be dead to the world at that time."

CHAPTER 59

Ruby

I should be happy. I mean, this is my wedding. That's what all the guests are here for. That's why I'm in this white gown sitting at the head table in this reception hall.

Funny. There's Jessi over there in a hideous maroon bridesmaid dress. There's no way either of us picked that one out.

Yup, this is definitely a dream.

Jessi's just given the toast and then says there's a slideshow before the dance. Pictures. This should be fun.

There I am opening presents on Christmas morning with Jessi and Mace because the heater went out in their house, and it was too cold for them to stay home.

There's the junior high summer camp we all went to, and there's the three of us in our matching tie-dyed T-shirts. A minute after they take this shot, Mace is going to throw me into the lake, and I'm going to be so mad I won't talk to him until dinner.

Now it's the Valentine's Day dance in ninth grade, the one where Mace brought me carnations and I cried because someone told me they were break-up flowers.

Mace at his high-school graduation. He's giving me a piggy-back ride, and I'm kissing him on the cheek, trying to knock off his hat and tassel.

The night before he went off to college and we stayed up until sunrise because we couldn't stand the thought of missing a single moment together.

And now I feel happy, just like I should since this is my wedding day.

But something's wrong. Jessi's screaming at the sound guy, "Turn that off. You can't show those here."

I want to finish the slideshow, but Jessi's mad. "Do you have any idea how rude this is? How do you think your husband will feel?"

And then I turn around. It's my own wedding dream, and I didn't even bother to check who the groom is.

It's not Mace.

The phone rings, and I'm awake.

CHAPTER 60

Mace

I've done it. I've made it nearly an hour by Jessi's side, and I haven't blown chunks once. If Ruby could see me now, she wouldn't have gone off about how selfish I am because I can't stand to be in the same room as my own sister.

I've been talking with the nurse, and she says for now I can stay here. There's a number I'm supposed to call tomorrow to get a room at the Ronald McDonald House. I guess it's not far. I can walk back and forth, but to be honest, tonight I'm glad I'm close by.

It's not like I could sleep anywhere else anyway.

Doctors have been in and out. I've got to be real careful when they come in that I don't get in their way or ask too many questions. It's the nurses who are the chatty ones, but sometimes even they get to working so hard that I know to leave them alone.

I've gotten a few more answers here, but I'm not sure

that's actually a good thing. My sister's basically covered in burns. Right now, since she's young and healthy, she's got a fifty percent chance of making it.

Which obviously means there's a fifty percent chance of her dying.

But I already told God he can't let that happen. And if God's real, then prayer works, and if prayer works, my sister's going to be fine.

But they've got this pamphlet here, something they give to family members, and it's pretty intense stuff. With burns this bad, Jessi might still be here by Christmas. Or even Valentine's Day.

They're talking about doing surgery tomorrow. Something to do with the skin.

I still have a hard time believing it's her. I guess that's a good thing. It'd be worse if I could see exactly what was under those bandages.

My poor sister.

A chaplain wants to come by and see me in the morning. A nurse already made the appointment. Seems kind of rude to me, I mean, just assuming I'd want to talk to someone like that.

But maybe if I get this chaplain to pray for Jessi to be healed, it'll make it happen that much sooner.

Honestly, I don't know how I'm going to make it through these next months. That's right. I said months. That's as long as a recovery like this is going to take. I asked one nurse, I said, "How is she supposed to lie here like this for that long?" and the nurse said, "You take it one day at a time."

I still don't see how that's going to help me get through all this.

I've been sitting by her bedside, and when the doctors and nurses aren't too busy, I talk to her.

"Hey, Jelly, remember when I convinced you to go on that tire swing out on the creek before it dried up? Remember when the branch cracked, and you fell in the water, and I got in big trouble? Dad was mad because he said I should have gone out on the tire swing first to test it. Make sure it was safe."

Jessi and me didn't have the best dad in the world, but he definitely wasn't the worst, and one thing he always told me was how I got to look out for my baby sister.

Test the branch before she does to make sure she doesn't get hurt.

So why's she the one all bandaged up with a breathing tube shoved down her throat, and why am I the one here staring at her?

I don't think she can really hear me, but the nurse said

it's kind of hard to know for sure, so I go ahead and talk to Jessi.

"Spent a little time with Ruby tonight. You should have seen how mad at me she was." I sigh. "I'm trying. I want us to be back together, but that won't ever happen until I believe in God, so you've got to get better because that was part of the deal I made with him. Hear me? You've got to get better."

Sometimes I cry, and the nurses pretend not to notice. I had no idea how much work they had to do. I guess one of the big things is giving Jessi a lot of liquids. They're talking about giving her some blood too. I tell the nurse I'll donate mine.

She says they've got a bank already.

So what am I supposed to do?

Just sit and wait, I guess.

The doctor's back. He's a real sour-looking one. You know Grumpy Cat online? Picture an old man with that same expression. That's the guy in charge. That's the doc taking care of my sister.

But he seems like he knows what he's talking about. Got to give him that.

Jessi's heart rate's all erratic. His words, not mine. And I guess that's got people pretty worried. I can't follow all the medical jargon, because seriously, who could? But I guess the basic idea is Jessi's body's working too hard, and they don't like that. There's something about her lungs getting burned too. I don't know if they mean from the inside or what, but the doctor frowns and tells me, "I'll do my best, but I'm not making any promises."

What are you supposed to say to that?

He heads on out, another nurse comes in, checks a few things, and goes out again. It's just me and Jessi.

I stare at my phone. It's too late to be calling anyone, but I don't know what else to do. I've talked to the doctor, I've talked to the nurses, I've talked to God and even my sister.

That only leaves one person left.

"Hey, Rubes. You sound terrible. Is something wrong?"

"It's okay. I was dreaming." She sounds groggy but not angry. That's a good sign. "How's Jessi? Is everything all right?"

"Yeah, she's okay. Got some weird heart thing going on the doctor's a little worried about, but other than that no changes. He said they'll do a surgery in the morning, but I don't know what."

"Probably a skin graft."

"A what?"

"Never mind. Did you call to fill me in?" She still sounds

like she's not fully awake, but at least she's not yelling at me. In the back of my head I've got this tiny question, like what if Jessi got herself hurt on purpose because she knew it would bring me and Ruby together again?

She's such a drama queen I can almost picture her doing it.

I know Ruby's waiting for an answer, so I say, "I wanted to see if you were okay."

"Do you have any idea what time it is?"

"Yeah." I knew calling her was a bad idea, but what choice did I have?

"Okay, well I'm going to go back to sleep now, and if anything changes …"

"Could you come over?" I blurt without really thinking through what I'm saying.

"Right now? I don't have a car."

"I'll call you a cab. Or an Uber. I could really use the company."

She's quiet, which is better than her saying no right away and hanging up. I wait.

"Where are you?" she finally asks.

"With Jessi. They're letting me stay here for the night. Can you come? Please?" I don't care if she thinks I'm a whining baby. I need her. Whether or not we're dating at the moment, she's got to know me well enough to realize that.

She sighs loudly. "All right. But let's plan to meet out in the lobby or something. I don't want to get in anyone's way."

"Deal."

I hang up the phone. This is literally the worst night of my life, but at least soon Ruby'll come cheer me up.

CHAPTER 61

Mace

She'll be here any minute, Ruby will. And it's a good thing. A second after I called the Uber for her, literally just a second, Jessi's monitor started beeping.

Something about that erratic heart again.

Now there's three nurses in here and even more monitors going off. I'm so tired at first I figure this must just be the way things go, but the nurses are all acting more worried than normal. It's my first indication something's wrong.

I think back to all those hospital movies and TV programs.

You never want to hear the monitors beep. Not like this.

"What's going on?" I ask.

The doctor's in here now too, the Grumpy Cat one. He doesn't even answer my question.

"What's going on?" I yell.

Someone tells me I need to leave. They need space to

work. Don't they realize this is my sister here?

More buzzing, more beeping, more nurses shouting at each other.

Holy cow. Is that one of those shock machines? I stare at the screeching monitor.

"Sir, you need to wait outside."

I hear the nurse but can't even understand what they're telling me.

That's my sister. I think the words but can't get them out.

Everyone's surrounding Jessi.

At least nobody else is trying to shoo me away.

There's so many bodies I can't even see what's going on at the bedside. I stare at the monitors. If Ruby were here she could tell me what all those numbers mean, except she'd do it in a way that made me feel stupid for not knowing myself.

Like I've ever gone to nursing school. Or would ever want to.

Something's changed. My head's so light I'm not even sure I'm breathing.

The numbers are still. Nothing's blinking anymore.

The nurses … What's different about the nurses?

They're all staring at the monitors too. Why aren't they paying attention to my sister?

"Let's try it again."

Try what? I don't know. More commotion, but not quite as loud as the first time.

The monitors don't change.

"Again?" someone asks, and I see the doctor shake his head.

A nurse pushes a button.

The monitor lies silent.

CHAPTER 62

Jessi

I have never been this hot before in my life. I'm burning up. And itching enough to drive myself mad. I want to scratch everywhere, but I can't move.

I try to gasp. Am I in hell?

Was Ruby right about everything?

I don't want to believe it. All I was trying to do was help Bowman. Dumb kid got himself shut in the bathroom. How many times did I tell him not to lock that door?

I tried picking the lock. That didn't work. I tried banging it with a plastic chair as if that would do anything. Stupid me, I could've grabbed the key from Denise's desk first, but when you've just had a stove explode in your face and you've had to herd a dozen kids outside and then there's one left stuck in a burning building, I'm not sure how clearly you're expected to think.

So I finally got Bowman out, and all the kids were

screaming and scared on the lawn, so I told them, "Calm down, everybody's fine. Everything's going to be okay," and I counted them to make sure there weren't any more missing.

And I remember thinking, "This is weird. Didn't that stove explode in my face? I wonder why I don't feel anything."

I feel it now.

I'm either on fire or I've died and gone to hell.

Ruby tried to warn me, her and that crazy old lady she takes care of.

Said if I didn't repent, this is what'd happen.

I hear voices around me. They're trying to get me breathing again.

Good, *I think. This isn't hell after all, even though it feels like it.*

There's a high-pitched beep in the background, and I put enough pieces together to realize what's happening.

Uh-oh. Not good.

Not good at all.

Because if I'm not dead yet, and this is how awful I feel, just think of what's going to happen to me if Ruby's right about eternity.

I force my brain to think. I've got to remember. What were the steps? Ruby even laid them all out for me one night when we were arguing about religion.

God, help, *I beg, even though it might be the very first time I've prayed and truly meant it.*

Truly expected an answer.

I need to remember what Ruby said.

Okay, first had something to do with sinning. I've got to tell God I'm sorry for all I've done.

I'm sorry! *I scream in my soul, and all around me more monitors are going off, and I think someone's trying to shock me back to life, but I don't feel any pain anymore. Just a tiny jolt.*

What did Ruby say the next step was? Come on, God. Help me remember.

Jesus is God's Son. That's right. I've got to believe Jesus is God's Son. I've got to really mean it.

I do! I believe everything.

All of it.

I believe in Jesus.

I believe in God.

I believe that everything Ruby said was true.

And I know I'm about to die so please, please, please don't send me to hell.

Have mercy on me. I know I don't deserve it, but those flames ... that heat ... Please forgive me. Please find me worthy enough. Please forget every single stupid mistake I made. Please don't punish me ...

It's quiet.

The nurses aren't yelling anymore.

Even the monitor has stopped.

I still don't hurt, but now I'm not afraid either.

It's like swimming in an ocean of peace.

And now I see him.

He's there.

He's real.

Just like Ruby told me.

I'm ready.

I'm forgiven.

I'm free.

CHAPTER 63

Ruby didn't mean to be late, but she'd gotten turned around when the Uber dropped her off in front of the parking garage, and she didn't have Elliot showing her the way.

Finally she made it. Eerie how quiet the hospital was at this time of night.

She kept looking over her shoulder, wishing she'd thought to pack her pepper spray.

The walls seemed to creak and groan, and half the lights were off. Dim shadows flickered down the empty hallways.

There was Mace.

Oh, no.

That look.

Oh, no. Please God ...

"You're late." She'd never heard him speak with such an expressionless tone.

It can't be true.

"You're late," he repeated. He balled his hands into fists.

"Mace, I'm so sorry ..." She hurried toward him but

stopped when she was close enough to see the rage in his eyes. He had never looked at her that way before, but she knew him well enough to know she shouldn't be here. Not right now.

She should get closer to the burn ward. Closer to people. *Help, God.*

He grabbed her arm before she could move. "Why didn't you come when I called you? It's too late now."

"I'm sorry. I'm so sorry." She glanced around, trying to find any exits nearby.

His fingers dug into her skin. "Sorry's not good enough. You were late, and now she's gone." He swung back.

Mace had never hit her before. Not a day in her life.

She fell, stunned, ready to kick him if he came any closer.

"What's going on here?"

A security officer? How did he get here so fast?

Mace knelt down by her.

"Sir," the officer bellowed, "Stand up and back away."

Ruby was too shocked to move. "I'm sorry," she whispered one last time, but her voice was so quiet even she could hardly hear it.

The man in the uniform crouched beside her. "Are you hurt? Do we need to get you medical attention?"

"I'm okay."

He turned to glower at Mace. "Do you know this man? We have counselors you can talk to. You can press charges."

She shook her head. "It's nothing like that. It's …"

Her throat seized shut, and an agonized sob welled up from the depths of her body.

The officer frowned. "Did he hurt you? Are you injured?"

She shook her head. She wouldn't even have a bruise.

The officer mumbled something into his radio. This was all a mistake. He thought she was crying because Mace knocked her down, but he was wrong.

She was crying for Jessi. For how terrified and scared she must have been in that fire. For how heroically she'd died, never even waking up long enough for anyone to thank her. For how many plans they'd made together that they'd never get to fulfill.

And not just Jessi either. Tonight she lost two best friends, not only one.

Mace would never recover from this. She had seen it clearly in his face before he stormed off.

He was so hurt and broken and childlike he needed someone to blame. He would never forgive Ruby for what happened.

Things would never be the same between them.

Not ever.

Two deaths instead of one.

How could she bear it?

How could she endure?

She continued to sob, and the officer just sat there on his haunches, listening to her wail.

CHAPTER 64

The next morning, Ruby sat with her coffee in the hospital cafeteria. It was early enough the workers were just starting to trickle in. The sun would be up soon.

Her first sunrise without Jessi.

Ruby had talked to the nurses. They didn't know where Mace was. Nobody had seen him since last night.

It was no surprise. Mace couldn't be expected to handle any of this.

The hospital staff wanted Ruby to make arrangements, but it wasn't her job. She had to drop her pretense and explain she wasn't really Jessi's sister-in-law.

Nobody gave her a hard time for lying.

She provided the nurses with the names and phone numbers of the relatives she knew of. Said she'd stick around until the afternoon just in case Mace showed up and they needed help handling him.

She should probably have been worried. He could've been out drinking or driving around recklessly or putting himself in all sorts of unimaginable dangers, but she wasn't his guardian. She couldn't control him.

She couldn't make him come to terms with his loss.

She had to let him go.

She hadn't cried except for that awful moment when the security officer came. Man, he must have thought she was a mess. The burn unit nurse asked if she wanted to meet with a chaplain, but Ruby wasn't ready for that.

Not yet.

She asked to see the body. Last night before Jessi died, the bandages had covered everything. It didn't look like her. But the nurse talked her out of it, said that seeing her best friend's body without the bandages was the worst possible idea.

Ruby had been too tired to argue.

And now here she was, wondering why she'd even told the staff she'd stick around until the afternoon. Mace wouldn't come back. There was no way he could face his sister's death like a responsible, mature human being. He was off running or drowning his sorrows at a bar or doing whatever he'd do.

She couldn't stop him.

It wasn't her job anymore. It should have never been in the first place.

She shook her head.

"So there you are."

She was so surprised at the voice she knocked her coffee over.

"I'm sorry." Elliot grabbed a few napkins off his tray and wiped up the mess. Thankfully, none had spilled on her clothes.

He gestured to the chair next to her. "Is this seat taken?"

She had to laugh. There were exactly two other people eating in a cafeteria that could accommodate hundreds.

"Got your note at the apartment," he said, then stared at her gently.

Could he read it in her eyes?

Did he know?

"Is everything okay?" he asked the question tentatively, like he was afraid to hear the answer.

She shook her head. The last thing she wanted to do was lose it here like she had in front of that security officer.

"Did Jessi have a bad night?"

Yeah. You could say that.

Why couldn't telepathy be a real thing?

"She didn't make it." Man, those words sounded so horrible coming out of her mouth.

"I'm sorry."

He was hugging her. She didn't want to cry, but what else was there to do? This was what she had needed from Mace.

This.

Someone to hold onto. Someone to talk to. Someone who wasn't afraid of her grief.

"Shh," Elliot whispered into the top of her head. "Shh. It's okay. You can cry for as long as you need. Take your time. Take all the time in the world."

CHAPTER 65

Now she understood why it'd been important to stick around. Ruby had been on the phone with Jessi's family all morning. She finally had to borrow a charger from one of the burn unit nurses. Who would have thought there were so many arrangements to be made when someone died?

The logistics gave her something to focus on. Elliot didn't know when he'd get a lunch break, but he was going to text her so they could spend a little more time together before she drove back to Orchard Grove.

Nothing was going to be the same without Jessi. Nothing at all.

But for now, she didn't have to worry about that. She had phone calls to make. Nurses who had questions she needed to answer. She told them she'd go ahead and talk to that chaplain, but he got called away on some other emergency and didn't show up.

Lunchtime came before she ever got her phone fully charged.

The cafeteria was far more crowded than it had been that morning, but there was Elliot, standing in the back of the line with his fresh green salad smiling at her.

She grabbed a bowl of clam chowder and joined him.

"How are you doing?" he asked.

She wasn't even sure how to answer.

And that was fine. With Elliot, she never felt hurried. Never felt like she had to pretend to be something she wasn't.

If she felt like a scared, confused, emotional ball of nerves, he was okay with that.

He could handle it.

She put her bowl of soup on his tray.

"What are you doing?" he asked.

She wrapped her arms around his waist and leaned her head against his sturdy chest.

He gave her the biggest squeeze he could considering how full his hands were.

She didn't let go until it was time to pay for their meals.

CHAPTER 66

Jessi's funeral was scheduled for the following Saturday, and Ruby wasn't ready.

Elliot invited her to stay in Seattle before jumping back to work at Orchard Grove. Ruby had considered his offer, but he would be so busy with work, she didn't have any idea what she'd do with herself.

She doubted Orchard Grove would ever feel the same without Jessi, but it was the closest thing she had to home.

Elliot would drive out Friday night so he could be there for Jessi's service and Grandma Lucy's birthday party.

The family didn't even know if Mace would come to the funeral.

Ruby tried not to worry about him, which was about as easy as if she'd tried to stop missing Jessi.

Connie wrapped her in a giant hug the second she stepped back home at Safe Anchorage Farms. "I'm so sorry about your friend," she whispered, and a minute later, Connie was the one crying, and Ruby was in the kitchen making tea trying to calm her down.

Grandma Lucy spent the rest of the week completely lucid, which was a mixed blessing. It was nice to have her back to her normal self, nice to have her praying all the time for Ruby's broken, aching soul, but it also meant Ruby had less work to do.

She even learned how to milk goats and work the cash register at the gift shop to try to pass the time.

Friday night came, and she sat in her room, thumbing through a journal Jessi's roommate had given her. "I think she would have wanted you to have this."

Reading Jessi's last journal was almost like hearing her best friend's voice in her ear again.

She laughed at some of the entries, like the one from last spring.

I swear, I don't know who I'm mad at more. My brother or Ruby for putting up with him. That boy will never grow up, especially if she keeps on babying him. I think she deserves so much better, but then I get selfish and know that there's nobody else I'd want as a sister-in-law. Maybe one day I'll tell her how I really feel, that Mace is never going to grow up and she should just move on and find someone better, but if I do that my brother'll kill me.

Talk about a dilemma.

Hearing Jessi's voice, even if it was only in her imagination, offered more healing than a dozen therapy sessions could.

The last entry was from four nights before the fire.

Ruby and I had another one of our long talks about God. I'm happy that she's found Jesus, but I'm trying to decide if it's for me. I still have some concerns. Like the fact that nearly every single Christian I know other than Ruby is thick-headed, stubborn, and just plain old mean. I definitely don't want to get like that.

But then there's that Grandma Lucy lady too. She's different than the rest. If I could become a Christian like her, that would be something else, except of course when the dementia sets in.

Like today when I went to pick Ruby up for a girls' night out, the old lady was still awake. She'd been having one of her off days, but she told me that I was going to walk through fire like those three guys in that Bible story from so long ago, and that Jesus would be right there with me.

Crazy old bat.

But Ruby and I had a good talk about religion, and I have a lot to think about. If Jesus really is the only way to get to heaven, I don't want to miss a chance like that.

Good thing I've still got time to sort things out.

Ruby didn't know if it was okay to pray for people who had already died, but she found herself begging God that Jessi had made the right choice in the end.

Any other option was too horrific to fathom.

It was dark out. She was rereading an earlier entry where Jessi was trying to decide how she felt with Ruby and Mace broken up when Connie called from downstairs.

"Ruby! Elliot's here to see you, hon. Come on down now."

It was surprising how her heart could be so heavy from grief, but it could still flutter at the thought of seeing Elliot again.

She glanced at herself in the mirror. With all the crying she'd done, it was a miracle she didn't look even worse. Oh, well. Elliot wasn't here for photo ops. She just had to keep on telling herself that.

He smiled as she came down the stairs. Seconds later, she was wrapped in those strong, safe arms again.

"That's a nice hug," he said.

"I missed you," she whispered.

Connie cleared her throat. "Don't stay up too late now, you two."

CHAPTER 67

Elliot was surprised when he first saw Ruby on the staircase. She looked years older. He'd seen grief do that before to his patients and their families, just not to someone he knew personally.

Then she hugged him, and everything felt as it should.

A few minutes later, they were rocking together on a porch swing in the back of the farmhouse. There was a slight breeze in the air, so he held her close, and they stared up at the stars.

It was hard to guess how long they'd been talking. Ruby had so many stories to share, stories about Jessi she didn't want to forget. If he'd thought it through, he would have brought a recorder so she could go back and listen to herself later. When the loneliness set in.

He took in a deep breath. "I wish I could have gotten to know her," he admitted. "Not many people find a best friend like that in a lifetime."

"I know." She snuggled against him a little more closely.

"I feel more lonely than I have in my whole life."

Elliot knew she was talking about more than Jessi. For all his faults, Mace had played an important part in Ruby's life. And from the sound of it, nobody had heard from him all week. They weren't even sure if he'd make it to his own sister's funeral.

Elliot knew all about loneliness, that heavy emptiness that sits like bricks in the center of your chest.

He wanted to alleviate some of that for her. Which is why he had to ask her this question.

He'd already run it by Tiff. He had to be certain he wasn't about to make the most stupid mistake of his life. He didn't want to scare Ruby away. But he didn't want to worry about her staying in Orchard Grove all alone either.

"I've been thinking about something," he began tentatively and cleared his throat. He needed to sound more confident. "Our office is looking for a nurse. It's pretty cush to be honest, regular day hours, nothing too physically demanding. I told the head that before he posted the opening online, I might have someone in mind."

She looked up at him.

"I know you've got your work here," he said, "and I don't want to take you away from a job you love, but after everything you've gone through, I was wondering if maybe a change of scenery would be healthy. A fresh start."

He worried he was being too forward, but he reached out and brushed her cheek with his thumb. Tucked a few stray strands of hair behind her ear.

"It would give us more time together too."

She blinked. "I don't know …"

"It's hard making any big decision when you're struggling with grief. I totally understand. And if this doesn't work out, there's always openings in Seattle. Just not maybe in the exact same department."

"Can I think about it for a day or two?"

He smiled. The fact that she was at least considering the position was a good sign. "My boss said he'd leave it open until Monday."

"That's really nice of you to think of me." She was still looking up at him with such trusting, expressive eyes.

He leaned a little closer to her and whispered, "Ruby?"

Her nose was close enough now to touch his. "Yeah?"

"I'm really glad we're together again." His lips brushed against hers. The breeze caressed them both.

And time had the decency to hold itself still while a goat bleated somewhere nearby.

CHAPTER 68

Ruby had no idea how she could have gotten through that entire service without Elliot. For the first time in her life, she knew what it meant to be by the side of a man who was supportive, strong enough to handle her emotions. Not like with Mace, where she was constantly looking out to make sure he wasn't about to make another immature mistake or throw a tantrum.

Mace had finally made his way to his sister's service halfway into the funeral. His eyes were bloodshot and his gait uneven as he staggered up to the front row.

She held her breath, praying he wouldn't make this any harder on the rest of the family.

Thankfully, he sat down and held his tongue.

So God really did answer prayers after all.

At least one of them.

At the reception, Elliot didn't let go of her hand. Or maybe it was the other way around. She needed him there. Needed his strength. Needed to be reminded that outside of

Orchard Grove was a world that still hinted at promises of hope and happiness. She could find her way there if she was patient enough with herself.

And Elliot seemed more than willing to be her guide.

She'd thought about his offer, and even though she was tempted at the idea of leaving Orchard Grove, with all its memories of Jessi's death, she couldn't leave Safe Anchorage. She couldn't do that to Grandma Lucy. He understood.

Elliot was a patient man.

He was more than willing to wait.

And she loved him for it.

At least she thought she did. Maybe it was too soon.

Maybe not.

She'd been thinking about it last night after he left for the hotel on Main Street. She'd never fallen in love before. With Mace, they'd known each other so long they basically grew up in love, or at least pretending to be.

This was different.

This was new.

She wanted more.

Elliot leaned down and whispered over the noise of the reception hall, "Got to run to the bathroom. I'll be back in a minute."

She glanced at the time. Connie wanted her back at Safe Anchorage to talk before Grandma Lucy's birthday party. Ruby was a little worried it had something to do with how late she and Elliot had stayed on that porch swing. Whatever it was, she couldn't stay here much longer.

She had to get back home.

She froze when she saw Mace heading straight toward her. "Hey."

She blinked at him and answered, "Hey."

"How's it going?" he asked.

"All right. How are you?"

He looked even worse up close. Had he slept at all this past week?

"I wanted to say I'm sorry." He stared at his feet. "For a lot of things. But especially that night when …" He blinked. "You know."

"Yeah." She couldn't quite meet his gaze. The pain in his expression was too intense.

"Did I hurt you?" he asked. "I can't even remember."

She shook her head. "I wasn't hurt."

"I'm glad." He shifted his weight. "I just, well, I guess that's all that's left to say."

She wanted to tell him to wait. Wanted to find some way to ask where he'd been, what he'd been doing. Lecture him for worrying his family like he did.

But Elliot was coming toward her now, and Connie had begged her to come home in time for that chat.

She had to go.

"Yeah," she repeated. "I guess that's all."

He gave a little nod to Elliot when he came up and mumbled, "Guess I'll see you later," and then he was gone.

CHAPTER 69

Elliot stood back while Connie nearly threw her arms around Ruby when they returned from Jessi's funeral.

Connie wiped her hands on the sides of her apron. "Oh, I'm so glad you got here when you did. The guests will be arriving any second, and we need to have a talk."

She pulled out a seat, but Elliot stood at the door uncertainly. "Should I go?"

"No, no, hon." Connie gestured to another chair. "You stay here too. This is hard news, and she's going to need someone she can rely on."

Elliot held his breath. More bad news? Could Connie have picked a worse day? How much more was someone as sweet as Ruby supposed to endure?

Elliot sat and held Ruby's hand. He scooted his chair a little closer to hers, as if he could offer her some extra strength by proximity. Whatever Connie had to say, he was going to be there for Ruby.

She sat perfectly still.

It's going to be all right, he wanted to tell her. Why didn't Connie get to the point? Instead, she sat there shaking her head, looking forlorn.

It was doing nothing to soothe Elliot's nerves. He could only imagine what Ruby must be going through.

"Well, now, you know when we hired you on here, we were waiting on the application through the state. We talked about that when you first took the job. Well, honey, I know this is awful timing with all you're going through right now. I've just been begging God all day to show me another way, but I got word they denied our application. Grandma Lucy has too many good days for them to recognize the need for full-time care. I don't see how we can keep you on here. I don't know what to do. I really don't."

Elliot glanced over at Ruby. Was that a smile she was trying to hide?

"It's all right, Connie. It really is," she said.

Elliot started to smile too.

Connie blew her nose loudly. "I just wish there was something I could do, something I could offer you."

Ruby squeezed Elliot's hand. "It's fine. In fact, I got offered a nursing position just last night."

Connie dried her eyes. "You did?"

"Yeah. I said I wasn't going to take it because Grandma

Lucy needed me here, but maybe this is God's timing anyway. Maybe I'm supposed to take this other job."

Connie clasped her hands together.

Elliot's heart felt fuller than it had in years.

"I'm so glad," Connie gushed. "You don't know how hard I was praying about what to do."

"What about Grandma Lucy?" Ruby asked. "Is she going to be all right here by herself?"

"Well, we've got a policy in this household and that's not to worry about things that we could focus our energy praying on. If Grandma Lucy keeps having good days, she's fine here. If her health gets worse, well ..." Connie glanced around and lowered her voice. "Maybe there's someone in the family who could come help a little bit. I'm sure we'll figure something out. That woman has more grandkids and great-grandkids than anyone can count. I'm sure there's someone out of all them who can take a little time watching her if it turns out we keep on needing full-time care. You know, maybe it's the medicine, but I really think she's getting better. Don't you?"

Connie's eyes shone with hope.

A similar hope to the one swelling in Elliot's chest.

"Yeah," Ruby answered. "I do."

CHAPTER 70

There must have been at least a hundred people who came out for Grandma Lucy's party. Ruby stayed by Elliot most of the time. It would be strange having to go out and make new friends now that Jessi was gone. All their lives, Jessi had arranged Ruby's social calendar for her.

After a small fiasco with a baby goat escaping the barn and running lose, Ruby and Elliot sat on the porch swing holding hands.

"I'm really glad you came here," she told him, wondering how hard both the funeral and this party would have been to face alone.

He leaned in a little, and she was reminded of their kiss last night.

"I'm glad too," he said. "It sounds like things really worked out for that new job, didn't they?"

"Yeah."

He frowned at her. "Why so pensive all of a sudden?"

"I think I'm going to miss it here." The words surprised

her. Now that Jessi was gone, Ruby would have thought leaving Orchard Grove would be the easiest decision she'd ever made. But all her memories were here. This was where she and Jessi and Mace had lived and grown up and loved each other and gotten into fights and made up.

It was scary to think of living and loving anywhere else.

"I talked to Tiff," Elliot was saying. "She says there's one or two apartments in her complex open for rent. It's not a bad part of town, and I think you two would really enjoy each other."

Ruby liked the idea of a built-in friendship, a social life she didn't have to go out and forge all by herself. "That sounds great."

There were so many things she wanted to ask him. What the new position would be like. How often they'd see each other. If it was a wise idea to take a job at the same place where your brand-new boyfriend worked.

He leaned his cheek against the top of her head and squeezed her hand. "I'm so glad I found you," he whispered.

She was too. Maybe God had known. Maybe Elliot was God's gift to make it easier for Ruby to say goodbye.

To Jessi.

To Mace.

To Orchard Grove.

She was scared of all the changes, but she'd have him Elliot lean on for support. And somehow, as they rocked in the soft autumn breeze, she had the feeling she was exactly where she was supposed to be.

She looked up at him.

"What?" he asked.

"Nothing."

"Why are you staring at me like that?"

"I was just thinking about last night."

He grinned. "What about last night?"

She tilted up her chin. Shut her eyes. Felt her lips melt into his.

She pulled away, cupping his slightly stubbly cheek with the palm of her hand.

"That's what I was thinking of."

He leaned back toward her. "Well, there's plenty more where that came from."

CHAPTER 71

Mace

It's the middle of summer and as hot as a desert. I haven't stepped foot in Orchard Grove in nine months, not since the funeral. Lame of me, you think? So sue me.

I'm actually doing a lot better than I was. Man, I was off the deep end for a while. When Jessi was in that hospital bed, I told her I couldn't live without her. Turns out I was almost right.

But here I am. Honestly, I wouldn't miss this for the world.

That stupid daycare's torn down completely, and it's never going to be rebuilt. Right here is now city land, and the mayor of Orchard Grove himself is about to name this little playground and picnic area after my sister.

The local hero.

The woman who saved a dozen children from a burning building.

I wish she could see this. Jessi would get a kick out of it all.

There's news vans out here, tons of people. I can't believe they're all here just for her.

I'm going to say a few words. I've been practicing with my sponsor. Yeah, I'm in a recovery group now. You don't want to know all the details, I'm sure, but losing my little sis was literally the worst possible torture I could have ever imagined. I almost didn't make it through, and I've got the scars to prove it.

Literally.

It'll be weird, talking in front of all these people, telling them how my sister was always like a hero. We haven't been in touch, but I assume Ruby'll be here too.

That'll be awkward.

Last I heard, she was dating that Seattle doctor. Sounds like they're getting pretty serious, at least if you were to go by all the pictures she puts up on social media of the two of them. Seriously. They're like the most photogenic couple in the world, and they know it. They may as well have been the ones to invent the couple's selfie.

I swear that rich doctor takes her everywhere. The state fair, day trips to the Oregon coast, baseball games, all kinds of theater shows … As if Ruby was ever into drama when we were together. She's just doing it for him, I'm sure.

They even went to the opera once and posted a dozen pictures of the two of them in their fancy getups.

Well, I'm happy for them. Really, I am. With as big of a wreck as I've been, I wouldn't have been there for Ruby like this doctor dude.

I know how to count my losses. I know how to be a good sport.

Which doesn't necessarily mean I'm excited to run into Ruby again, to get reminded of everything I lost in addition to my sister, but you can't change the past. I swear if I had a penny for every time my recovery sponsor made me say those words … Oh, well. I'm clean now. Doing all right. I've been working pretty steady at a Starbucks in Spokane. It's not the best job, but they have all right benefits for what it is. Never did finish that sixth year of college, but my sponsor's got me applying to a few different online programs, and we're going to see which ones will transfer the most credits over.

So in a couple months, that might make me a seventh-year senior.

Wouldn't Jessi be proud?

There's Ruby. I see her getting out of that slick car. Man, what I wouldn't give for a ride like that. Well, I'm not going to get that whipping up frappes at Starbucks, am I?

But if she's in that fancy of a get-up, that means he's here too. Guess I shouldn't be so surprised. I just hope they don't rub their lovey dovey photogenic happiness in my face, know what I mean?

She sees me and offers a kind of awkward wave. She's probably trying to guess if I'm about to knock her over like I did the night Jessi died. I swear I've never hit a girl before and never will again. I still don't know what came over me. My sponsor tells me it was the grief, that I have to show myself a little bit of grace, but that's the one thing I've done in my life I'll never be able to forgive.

There's her boyfriend, the doctor dude. If you want my opinion, he looks like a boring stiff. But maybe that's her type now.

The mayor's about to speak. At least I don't have to talk to Ruby right now. I can do it after the ceremony. Or maybe I'll just go away real quick after everything's done.

It's one of those things where we'll just have to see how it goes.

CHAPTER 72

Elliot squeezed Ruby's hand. "You ready for this?"

She nodded. She could hardly remember Jessi's funeral. Now a full nine months had passed. She was glad to be here.

Glad to honor Jessi's memory like this.

She was so thankful to have Elliot here by her side and so proud of her friend.

After the small ceremony dedicating the brand-new Jessi Lacasa Park, Ruby and Elliot would have a quiet lunch at Safe Anchorage and then drive back to Seattle. He was so busy building up his own practice now that he'd finished his residency, the drive was one of their first real chances to connect in weeks.

When Elliot started his own business last spring, Ruby ended up staying at the old office. She'd made quite a few good friends with the other staff there, and his new place was still in the same wing of the hospital, so they could have lunch together every day and carpool to and from work.

She leaned against Elliot's strong, sturdy frame as the

mayor made his opening address and then invited Mace to the podium to share a few words.

Ruby was surprised. For as long as she'd known him, she'd never seen Mace speak in public before.

She hadn't seen him since the funeral. She hoped it wouldn't be too awkward once the ceremony ended. There was something she wanted to give him. She'd talked it over with Elliot, and he thought it was a good idea too.

She just hoped it wouldn't send Mace back off the deep end.

He looked like he was doing all right. He'd put on some weight, which was a good thing. A little bit better color too, like maybe he had finally learned how to have a life that didn't involve sitting indoors playing video games twenty hours a day.

"My sister was no hero," he began and jumped right into one of Jessi's most embarrassing stories of being in the middle of a shower during a power outage and running out in a towel with her soapy hair, not realizing that her brother had invited over several of his friends from college.

Ruby clutched Elliot's hand even tighter. What was Mace thinking? Did he have any respect?

Any human decency?

"She was no hero," he repeated, "or at least that's what

she thought."

Ruby began to relax, but only slightly.

"Jessi was working at the Play'n'Learn Daycare when a gas leak caused an explosion. I'm sure we all know the story by now, how even though she had the most severe burns of them all, she made sure to get all the kids outdoors to safety and then even returned to the burning building to rescue a little boy.

"I know my sister pretty well, and I'm guessing she didn't wake up that morning and ask herself if she was ready to die to save someone else. I'm sure when she ran back into the daycare, even with all the injuries she'd already suffered, she wasn't asking herself if it was really worth it to go back in. She did what she had to do. If we're going to be totally honest, she didn't even like her job all that much."

Ruby swallowed down a groan. *Don't tell them that, Mace.*

Too late now.

A few members of the crowd chuckled. Hopefully they'd think he was making a joke.

"But she was a hero nonetheless, even though she never knew it. I'm glad Orchard Grove is putting up this park in her honor, because there's literally not a better sister or a better daycare worker or a better human being in the entire world who deserves this park to be named after her more than Jessi does."

He stepped down from the podium to the sound of polite applause, and Ruby kept on holding Elliot's hand, counting down the minutes until she was free to give Mace the package she'd brought.

CHAPTER 73

Elliot had reservations about Ruby talking to Mace at the park dedication. How could she be certain it was safe? The night Jessi died, Mace had attacked her, and it took a security officer just to pry him off her.

But Elliot also sensed the compassion behind Ruby's plan and in the end was fully supportive.

"You ready?" he asked as the crowd started to disperse. "You got it?"

She glanced at her purse. "Yeah. It's here."

"Okay. I'll wait in the car. I've got a new book on my phone, so take your time." When Elliot wasn't working or spending time with Ruby, he was researching business strategies for running his own oncology practice. He went into medicine to heal people, but now he had to act as a CEO, entrepreneur, and, until he found more staff, he was his own HR department too.

Good thing Ruby was patient. She never complained about the crazy hours he kept, and several nights a week she'd come over after her shift to help him with some of the seemingly endless amounts of busywork.

It was nice that they had the extra time together, but he didn't want to take advantage of her giving nature any more than necessary.

His hectic schedule had certainly taken its toll on their relationship. This drive out to Orchard Grove was the first time they'd had to just sit and talk in nearly a month.

They needed to spend more time together. That was all there was to it.

Which is why he was so convinced that he was making the right decision.

He'd talked it over with Tiff just to make sure it wasn't too soon. But he and Ruby had been dating for nine months, and especially with him in the last stages of starting up his own practice, now seemed the best time.

He'd bought the ring weeks ago. Tiff went with him to pick it out, and since she and Ruby were so close now, he trusted her judgment implicitly.

And now he was less than an hour away from giving it to her. He planned to propose at Safe Anchorage, felt it would be fitting to have Grandma Lucy there to give her blessing since she'd played such a big role in both of their spiritual lives and in bringing them together.

He hoped he wasn't so nervous he'd forget all that he'd planned to say.

He watched her from the car window. After the fire, Ruby got hold of the journal Jessi kept before she died. Now it was time to pass it on to Jessi's brother.

Elliot hoped it might give the poor kid some of the peace and healing he needed. He watched from the Tesla while Ruby leaned over and gave Mace a quick hug. Then she turned and started walking toward the car.

So that was that.

"You ready?" she asked, sitting down beside him with a smile he'd grown to love.

He was so nervous he wasn't even sure he'd make it all the way until after lunch like he'd originally planned. He might just drop to his knee on the front porch and ask her there.

He squeezed her hand. "Ready." What had he ever done to convince God he deserved someone like her?

Just a few more minutes and they'd be at Grandma Lucy's. He pictured how surprised Ruby would be.

How happy.

How beautiful.

He pictured their future, caring for their patients and then coming home and refreshing themselves in the love they shared together.

Filling each other up so they could wake up the next morning and keep on serving others.

It was a beautiful, glorious picture.

His Tesla couldn't speed them to Safe Anchorage fast enough.

FROM THE AUTHOR

I hope you enjoyed Ruby and Elliot's story! One thing I love about writing romance is the way these novels remind me what it was like when my (now) husband Scott and I were getting to know each other (and falling HARD for each other in spite of being long-distance).

Christian romance is unique because it dives into something so much deeper than physical attraction … the spiritual lives of the characters.

When Scott and I met, he was living in LA and I was a college student on the East Coast. By the time he called me on the phone and told me he was falling in love with me, he hadn't even seen my picture, but we were both certain God had ordained for us to be together.

Even though our story has the perfect ingredients for a happily ever after, we've still struggled like so many other Christian couples. Miscarriages, depression, a baby in the NICU … these aren't just the trials we faced as newlyweds. They're also the backdrop for the Orchard Grove Women's

Fiction series.

Return to Orchard Grove, except now it's not about couples finding the love of their lives. It's about strengthening relationship in spite of hurts and tragedy.

It's Christian fiction that's about as true to real life as you'll get without stepping inside someone else's shoes. But even though the struggles might be real, the God who works redemption throughout every page of these novels is bigger than any trial (real or fictitious) life might throw at you.

Dive into the Orchard Grove series to meet women who discover God is bigger and stronger than the struggles they face. Readers have called the novels in this series "the best of all Alana's books," "probably the most thought-provoking book I've ever read," and "a book I'll never forget."

Book reviewer Kim P once admitted, "If I could, I would give copies to every woman I know." This entire series is jam packed with inspiration and encouragement for your Christian journey (as well as some hard-hitting Biblical truths and nourishment for the soul straight from the mouth of Grandma Lucy).

Take a step closer to God when you read the Orchard Grove Christian today. Use code NEXTPLEASE to save on your next Alana Terry novel from christianbooks.today!

www.ingramcontent.com/pod-product-compliance
Lightning Source LLC
Chambersburg PA
CBHW060657190726
48289CB00002B/455